No Way Back

Cole Rickard is returning to the Arizona town of Maverick, where he is hoping to make amends for an ignominious departure five years previously. His status as the Reno Kid, a ruthless bounty hunter and fast gun, has made him the target of young hotheads eager to snatch away what he now considers to be a crown of thorns.

But shucking such a dubious reputation is tough: there will always be somebody waiting to call him out and many will have no qualms about using underhanded tactics. Will Cole ever be allowed to settle down to the life of domesticity he now craves with his estranged wife and son? Or will there be no way back for the Reno Kid?

No Way Back

Ethan Flagg

A Black Horse Western

ROBERT HALE · LONDON

© Ethan Flagg 2015
First published in Great Britain 2015

ISBN 978-0-7198-1679-6

Robert Hale Limited
Clerkenwell House
Clerkenwell Green
London EC1R 0HT

www.halebooks.com

Typeset by
Derek Doyle & Associates, Shaw Heath
Printed and bound in Great Britain by
CPI Antony Rowe, Chippenham and Eastbourne

ONE

DARK IN THE AFTERNOON

The hot sun shone down from a cloudless sky of deepest blue. Sitting astride a sorrel mare, the rider removed his black Stetson and wiped a sleeve across a sweat-beaded brow. His hand strayed to the water bottle hanging from the saddle horn. A tongue like tough cinch leather filled his mouth making it difficult to swallow. It reminded him too late that more than one water bottle was essential in this bleak country. He shook it.

The turgid slosh indicated there was insufficient to slake his raging thirst. But just enough to revive his flagging mount. In this harsh and arid land, the last thing a man needed was to be cast afoot. His horse had to come first.

Dismounting, he emptied the tepid contents onto his bandanna and rubbed the sorrel's muzzle, squeezing the remains into the open mouth. The animal snickered in appreciation. Its noble head quivered as the life-giving elixir was gratefully imbibed.

'Not much further, old gal,' he murmured into the twitching nostrils. A note of concern crept into the optimistic assessment of his grim situation. 'At least I hope not.' Eyes squinted in the bright sunlight as he peered across at the bleak expanse of endless sand and rock.

He leaned down and picked up a pebble, popping it into his mouth. This would have to do until he could find water. A poor substitute but enough to stimulate a few drops of saliva to keep him going.

That was the claim from an old prospector he had encountered up in the Mogollon country two days before. The sourdough miner had been working a creek with his rocker box. He had shared his meagre rations with the traveller, airing some much appreciated snippets of advice for survival in this harsh terrain. The pebble trick was one such. Only time would tell if it worked.

Stretching the stiffness from tired muscles, the rangy guy ran a hand through his thick black hair, scraping it back off his forehead.

Age was fast coming up on the outside to overtake him. Clear evidence was the streaks of grey that had become far too well established. Lines akin to a ploughed field creased his tanned features making him look a decade older than his thirty-six years.

He pushed back his hat and fingered the livid scar on the side of his head, remembering how it had been acquired. Someday he would find the conniving rat who had caused it.

The trail-weary appearance was not just the result of Arizona's unforgiving climate. Cole Rickard was a bounty hunter. A profession, if such it could be termed, that took its toll on the men who chose this precarious way of life. Shunned by both sides of the law, these men had to be constantly on their guard.

But the rewards could be high. It was the lucrative payouts that kept most manhunters in the game. That and the excitement of the chase were addictive, not to mention the kudos of acquiring the reputation of a fast gun.

Very few of these knights of the frontier survived to reach old age. There was always going to be somebody just that little bit faster on the draw. Young pretenders, always eager to snatch the crown from the current King Colt. Yet still they clung to the illusory belief of being invincible. A fatal blend of arrogance and mule-headedness that invariably cost them dear.

Cole Rickard was the best, and the most feared of the bounty men. But that did not stop reckless hotheads from calling him out. Boot Hill cemeteries across the West were filled with those who had tried and failed. He had once attempted to figure out how many, but had given up when the tally reached double figures.

Now he was heading back to the town of Maverick in Arizona's San Carlos Valley. He had been away for five long years. Another four days should see him there. Home at long last. He could hardly wait. At least, he hoped it would still be his home. There were no guarantees that he would be made welcome.

A fervent anticipation that he could make a fresh start had persuaded him to take this little-used but direct trail across the Natanes Plateau. He was beginning to think it would have been a sight easier and quicker to have taken the longer route by way of Tucson. Too late for regrets now. He was committed.

Known as the Reno Kid, he wanted out of the gunfighting caper. Just plain Cole Rickard would suit him fine. If only he could finally bury that reputation. Once regarded as an exciting adventure, it was now like an albatross hanging round his neck. All he craved was to make amends for past indiscretions and to settle down once again with his wife and son.

And this time it would be for good. His mind was made up.

At one time such a life would have seemed dull and mundane. Domestic drudgery fit only for poor suckers who had no ambition. Yet now it was all he yearned for. The regular pattern of familial routine beckoned invitingly. No more constantly looking over your shoulder waiting for the next challenge. But it all depended on whether Marcia would have him back.

Young Joey would be eight years old now. How had he faired during the time his wayward pa had been absent? Was he doing his school work and helping his ma with the household chores? Had Marcia managed to keep him on the straight and narrow without the guiding hand of a father? All these questions and more were what Cole yearned to have answered.

He shook his head at the idiotic notions that had led him into the foolhardy lifestyle where a six-shooter was his tool of trade. Sure, it had brought him plenty of dough, most of which had been frittered away, and a reputation that saw men step aside when he walked down the street. Excitement in abundance with the thrill of danger that the next pursuit would bring.

But had it all been worth it? That was the question now dogging his troubled mind. At the age of thirty-six, he had grown up. Taking on young gunslingers who sought to wrest a hard-won status no longer seemed important. Indeed, it was becoming increasingly irksome. The Reno Kid was still well capable of holding his own in any gunfight, yet he knew that sooner or later some dude would best him. It was inevitable. No reputation could last for ever.

Reno sensed his comeuppance was fast approaching. A leery smirk creased his gaunt features. The Reno Kid! And they still called him that, even though he was well past any association with his youth.

It had been acquired from a town marshal in the Nevada town of that name after bringing in the second owlhooter that month. Sarcasm loosely disguised as envy had prompted the old lawman to announce, 'The Reno Kid strikes again. Don't spend all that dough in the same candy store.'

The marshal's attempt to unsettle the newly commissioned young manhunter failed. Cole Rickard liked the sound of it. And so the Reno Kid was born.

But a lot of water had flowed down the creek since those thrilling early days when the world was his oyster. He dismounted and sat down on a rock beside an old juniper tree. The gnarled roots, twisted and warped like a tangled ball of string, reminded the ruminating traveller of his own churned up innards.

A smoke would help ease the tightness in his guts. Cole hooked out the makings and rolled himself a quirly. Drawing the smoke deep into his lungs helped to focus his thoughts as he cast back to how it had come to this depressing state of affairs.

The Reno Kid's encounter with the lovely Marcia Kemp had been at the monthly hoedown in Maverick back in '73.

He had recently delivered an outlaw to the sheriff's office. Wanted in three states for murder and robbery, Kansas Bob Jacket was worth a cool thousand dollars. Reno had been trailing him for two months, finally catching up with the critter in the Arizona badlands north of Safford.

The hunter had caught Jacket, literally, with his pants down. Reno couldn't contain his delight at catching the notorious bandit thus encumbered. Even though considerably disadvantaged in his moment of personal relief, Jacket had refused to come quietly. A hangman's rope was awaiting him following the inevitable guilty verdict from the twelve good men and true. Knowing Reno's reputation did not deter him from making his play.

'Sooner go down in a blaze of glory than choking at the end of a rope,' was his final response to the bounty hunter's chuckling encouragement to surrender.

The result was as expected. Dead or Alive, as it said on the poster, made no difference to the Reno Kid. Bob Jacket had opted for the former and paid the ultimate price. In fact it was far easier if these brigands did balk at getting arrested. A dead outlaw was much easier to handle than one always searching for a way out on the long ride to incarceration.

That was not the choice of receiving lawmen who lost the opportunity of an extra fee earned from a trial.

'I been hearing about how you bring all your marks in over a saddle, Kid,' the sardonic lawman jeered. If truth be told, Sheriff Chalk Fenton held a sneaking admiration for these guys. It irked that he himself did not have the bottle demanded of such a lifestyle. 'News like that spreads quickly.'

The bounty hunter fixed a jaundiced eye on the speaker. He had heard this quibble numerous times before.

'This *hombre* was given the chance to quit, Sheriff.' He gave the comment a nonchalant shrug. 'Ain't my fault he made the wrong choice.' He held out his hand. 'Now if'n you don't mind, it's been a thirsty ride. Which is the best drinking parlour in town?'

Fenton huffed some but had no option but to pay up. 'Hell's Acre is the right joint for jaspers of your calling.' With a sneering reluctance born of jealousy, Fenton paid the bounty hunter off. This was more dough than a humble lawdog could earn in a month of Sundays.

Reno casually flicked through the wad of green-backs. A half-smile creased his handsome features. 'Looks like it's all there. Much obliged, Sheriff. I'll make sure not to spend it all at once.' A patronizing smirk left the tinstar fuming helplessly as Reno exited the office.

The bounty hunter fully intended to avoid the recommended drinking den known as Hell's Acre. Ambling down the main street, it was the Buckeye that caught his attention due to its well-maintained exterior. A fresh paint job and clean windows beckoned invitingly. He was not disappointed..

Cole had hung around Maverick for a few more days. Sheriff Fenton would have much preferred the bounty hunter to move on, but unless he broke the law, the starpacker was powerless to act. Cole took a room at the National Hotel. He liked the town. And the people seemed friendly enough. Within a week he reverted to his God-given name of Cole Rickard to help allay any suspicions as to his intentions.

Marcia Kemp came into his life at the next Saturday dance. She was a breath of fresh air in an otherwise sordid existence. Cole began to realize that there was more to life than strutting his stuff about town gaining attention through the creation of fear and awe.

The handsome school ma'am was flattered by the attentions of the good-looking stranger in their midst. Soon they were walking out. After three months of courtship, they were married. A child inevitably followed.

By seeking out this remote backwater, Cole was confident of having covered his steps. Only by a freakish accident could anybody find him here. And as time passed, so his notoriety would likewise fade into oblivion. His dubious earnings from the Jacket bounty enabled him to buy a half share in the Buckeye saloon.

Flush Harry Donovan was well aware of Reno's reputation but respected his desire to forge a new life far removed from his gunslinging days. Although it was never mentioned, other issues played their part in his enthusiastic welcome of the ex-manhunter into the business. Reno's past reputation would act as a tempering influence on those who might have otherwise caused trouble.

As his nickname suggested, Donovan ran the gambling side of the business. His penchant was for poker, always seeming to favour a Royal Flush hand.

Had Cole known about his partner's surreptitious motive, he might well have sought an investment elsewhere. It was Donovan's clandestine use of his partner's professional infamy that was to have devastating consequences.

TWO

BLAST FROM THE PAST

For three years everything ran smoothly.

The saloon prospered, young Joey was growing up into a fine boy and most of all, his love for Marcia strengthened with each passing day. Yes indeed, life could not have been better for Cole Rickard. The Reno Kid had finally been laid to rest. A bright future looked assured.

Many of the current residents of Maverick knew nothing of his violent past. Even Sheriff Chalk Fenton had softened his attitude to the notorious gunslinger now living in his town.

Cole felt safe and secure. But it was all an illusion, a tantalizing chimera. And just as night follows day, the bubble was sure to burst. He ought to have realized that a hard-bitten reputation such as that attained by

14

the Reno Kid would never truly be expunged. And so it came to pass one fine July afternoon in 1876.

Cole was discussing with his partner the idea of expanding the business to include a theatre and dance hall. The premises adjacent to the Buckeye had recently become vacant and would make the perfect venue for attracting top entertainers from around the country. It would also provide an ideal venue for the monthly hoedowns, at present held in barns dispersed throughout the valley.

They were about to work out some figures in the office when a cutting retort sliced through the general conversation of men drinking and playing cards. This was no ordinary hollering, but aimed specifically at Cole Rickard. A hoarse growl, jarring on the nerves, it instantly silenced the inane jabbering. All eyes turned towards the sudden interjection.

A large bear of a man stood framed in the doorway, his profile a dark silhouette.

'It's taken me a long while to catch up with you, Reno,' the man snarled. 'Now fill your hand and let's get to shooting.'

Doyle, the burly tough, hunkered down into the gunman's stance, his hands hovering above the twin Smith & Wesson .44s.

The name Reno didn't immediately strike a chord with the saloon's patrons. Furrowed brows displayed mystification. What was this guy claiming? Puzzled eyes swung between the two participants.

One man whispered what all the others were now thinking. 'Is Cole Rickard really none other than the

Reno Kid?' Gasps circulated as the import of what had been suggested took hold like a wild bush fire.

'But I thought he only operated up north,' mouthed another drinker.

Nods of agreement responded to this poignant comment. But it was Doyle who confirmed what was merely a piece of idle speculation.

'That's right, boys,' he rasped out in answer to their baffled expressions. 'You've been living with that lowlife skunk in your midst all this time. This turkey is none other than the Reno Kid. But not for much longer. You ready for this, Reno?'

A brief moment of silence hung heavy in the long narrow room as the implications of the assertion struck home. Then, as one, chairs scraped and tumbled over as the patrons sought to remove themselves from the field of conflict. Tables were upended as men took cover on the floor. Within seconds, only Cole Rickard and his partner were left standing as the challenger moved inside the saloon.

Flush Harry swallowed. He had lived in dread of this happening.

Using the Kid's name to scare off trouble was something he now bitterly regretted. The incident in question had occurred one Saturday night. Some drunken cowhands were passing through on their way back from a trail drive. They had been threatening trouble when some of the girls had denigrated their lecherous suggestions. Donovan had mentioned the name of the Reno Kid being in town and that he was a good friend. That piece of news soon curbed their unwelcome passion.

The man himself, however, had been in Globe at the time on business.

The cowboys must have spoken of the incident to others. Such talk gets around. Passed on from mouth to mouth by saddletramps and drifters. Donovan rightly assumed that talk of the incident had come to the ears of Wesco Doyle. This was not the first time that Cole's partner had played the Reno card. But it was the first time it had brought more trouble than he could ever have imagined.

The gambler quickly shrugged off his shocked reaction. 'You know this guy, Cole?' he asked in a voice crackly and shaking due to the tension of the moment.

'Never met him before,' came the terse reply. So intent was he on watching the movements of this man mountain that his partner's jumpiness washed over him.

The newcomer moved across to the bar. Eyes glued to his quarry, the big man snatched up a bottle standing on the counter and tipped a hefty slug down his throat.

A sarcastic chortle greeted the denial. 'The name's Wesco Doyle. You know my brother, Leroy. Or should I say you did until you shot him down.' Doyle's voice was growing louder in conjunction with his rising anger. 'I've been tracking you for over three years. Figured the scent had gone cold. Then I heard your name mentioned up north in Snowflake.'

Doyle took another long slug of hooch then nonchalantly tossed the bottle across the room. Gasps of fear and alarm issued from numerous throats as the bottle smashed against an iron post. The gunman never batted an eyelid.

'Well I'm here to see that justice is finally done. A varmint that shoots a guy in the back ain't no better than a snake in the grass. But I ain't like you, Reno. So I'm giving you an even break. Now are you gonna take me on, or is that a yellow streak I see painted across your miserable brow?'

A muttering could be heard from the cowering patrons of the saloon. If one thing was likely to incense frontiersmen it was backshooting. And the accusation was aimed squarely at the man they had all come to admire and respect.

Cole immediately sensed that he had to act quickly. His hard-won reputation as an upright citizen was in jeopardy of being wiped out. And it was due to a mistake he had hoped was long since buried.

How could he ever forget the shooting of Leroy Doyle?

That was the only time the Reno Kid had ever shot an adversary in the back. And it had haunted him ever since. Leroy was just another young hothead who had tried to gain the reputation as the man who shot the Reno Kid. The unforgettable incident had occurred six months before Cole had arrived in Maverick. The mining camp of Telluride up north in Colorado was the fateful setting.

But it was Doyle who had tried to shoot *him* in the back.

A warning from the barman had averted certain

death by the merest whisker as the bullet had scraped Reno's ribcage. Attuned to instant reactions, the bounty hunter had swung on his boot heels, drawing his own revolver and snapped off two shots at the bushwhacker. Doyle had been turning to flee the scene of his contemptible skulduggery when he was drilled squarely in the back.

Nobody blamed Reno. His reactions had been instinctive. Everybody in Telluride agreed that Doyle had deserved his plot on Boot Hill. Clearly, though, there was one person who held a grudge. And he was now standing here in Maverick.

Wesco Doyle was urgently seeking to even the score. And it was obvious that no amount of excuses would satisfy him. The guy wanted blood. Not the life-giving force running through Cole Rickard's veins, but the blood of the Reno Kid. And now that the sorry episode had been resurrected, the clientele of the Buckeye would also expect a spirited response from such a notable gunfighter.

Backing down would turn him into a pariah within the community. His name would be reviled and trailed through the mud. The Reno Kid had to stand firm and meet the challenge head on to enable Cole Rickard to maintain his standing in the Maverick community. It was Flush Harry who butted in on his thoughts.

'There's no need for any shooting, mister,' Donovan appealed, hoping to calm the irate bruiser down. 'Let's sit down over a drink and talk this through.'

'I ain't come all this way to jaw,' rapped Doyle. 'Now

19

move out the way if'n you don't want some of the same.'

'Best do as he says, Harry,' Cole advised pushing his friend back. 'This turkey is in no mood for listening to reason.'

Donovan was relieved to get out of the firing line. But he tried one more tack to prevent certain bloodshed. 'The sheriff won't take kindly to gunplay in this town. You'll be arrested.'

Again Doyle laughed. It had a hollow ring. 'No lawdog is gonna interfere with a hogleg contest. That's the unwritten law of the West. There ain't a judge in the territory who would convict the winner of a one-on-one challenge where both parties are in agreement.' He sneered at the man he knew only as the Reno Kid. 'There is another way out, of course. The sneaking rat could always walk away with his tail between his legs. Is that how it's gonna be, backshooter?'

Cole was sweating. His hackles were rising. Being labelled a backshooter and a coward were insults that could have only one outcome. The problem was that he had not fired a gun in anger for three years. Could he handle a practised gunman like Wesco Doyle and come out on top? The guy was obviously adept. Nobody wore a twin rig like that unless he could use it.

His hands flexed. They felt stiff. Or was that just nervous tension?

With slow deliberation he raised his arms. 'I ain't carrying, Doyle.'

It was a futile attempt to gain some much needed

time to gather his wits together for the inevitable show-down.

In slow motion, the gunman purposefully lifted one of the pistols from its holster and slid it along the bar. The shiny revolver settled ominously, six inches from Cole's resting hand.

'You have now,' leered Doyle squaring his broad shoulders. 'We've wasted enough time already. Now get to shooting, or crawl away on your ass.'

At that moment the saloon door burst open. Emitting a cry of alarm, a woman rushed into the room. It was Marcia Rickard. She dashed over to where her husband was standing.

'Aveline Beddows was passing the saloon when she saw what was happening. It's lucky I was close by. You have to stop this now,' Marcia pleaded grabbing her husband's arm. 'What happened before you came to Maverick is all in the past. It's the future that matters now. Our future. Joey's future.'

The words tumbled out as the comely woman tried desperately to avert a catastrophe. 'You are a husband and a father now, Cole. I don't want my son growing up knowing his father is a killer. Or worse still, that he has no father at all. Is that what you want?' She hurried on, not giving him chance to speak. 'Stop this now and come away before it's too late.'

She clawed at her husband's sleeve, the earnest appeal willing him to see reason.

But it was to no avail and fell on deaf ears. Cole's frosty regard was glued firmly to the challenging hulk of Wesco Doyle. Without shifting his look, he gently prised his wife's hand off.

'Too late for that, Marcia. The cards have been dealt and I have to play this hand to a conclusion. Winner takes all. There's no other choice.'

'This isn't a game, Cole,' snapped the petrified female. 'There's always a choice. You can walk away right now and nobody will think any the worse of you.'

'You gonna hide behind a woman's skirts, Reno?' Doyle goaded his adversary. 'That would sure be the action of a backshooter.'

Cole bristled angrily. His normally placid temper was rapidly shredding at the edges. A look chock full of venom speared the hovering gunman. Then, with slow deliberation and breathing deeply, his gaze shifted to his beautiful wife's gravely beseeching countenance. 'You know that ain't true, Marcia. A man has to be able to hold his head up. Life wouldn't be worth a dime in Maverick if'n I were to walk away from this now.'

The whole saloon was hanging on his every word. He could see nods and grunts of accord. He would be labelled a coward, no better than a rabid cur.

No man could live with that hanging over him. At best he and his family would have to up sticks and leave Maverick. But things like that were apt to follow a man round. Wherever he went, whispered voices and point-ing fingers would mark him out as the cocky gunslinger with the yellow streak.

Marcia tried one last tack to persuade her beloved husband that his paternal responsibilities overshad-owed all else. Her declaration was pitched low and even, but fizzled with suppressed emotion. 'Go through with this, Cole, and you could end up dead. But whatever happens, I could not live with a man who put stubborn arrogant pride above duty to his family. Joey is staying with Aveline at the moment. If you insist on continuing on this road to destruction, you will never see him again.'

She gave him one last look, an imploring petition that tugged at the ex-manhunter's heartstrings. Sure it did. Who but a stone-hearted moron could not be so moved? And he dearly wanted to turn his back on Wesco Doyle and join his wife.

And he almost did just that. Marcia's threat was no idle throwaway. She meant every word.

On the other hand, Cole Rickard was a man of gentle and insistent persuasion. He had done it before. Why not again? Surely she would not reject all they had built up in Maverick. Yet in his heart, he knew that she was serious. Continue with this life or death struggle, and he could say goodbye to all he held dear.

But once again, the shame of backing down and being branded a craven milksop raised its ugly head. His mind was made up. There was no other way. The straight back stiffened, shoulders squared as a hard glint showed in the staring eyes.

He signalled to Harry Donovan to remove his wife from the field of battle. His partner quickly hustled the crying woman away. Her sobs had fallen on deaf ears.

'Now make your play, Doyle. I'm ready anytime you are.'

The gunman dug into his pocket and extracted a silver dollar. He placed it on the thumb of his left hand intending to flick it into the air. 'When this coin hits the floor, go for your piece. Agreed?'

Reno nodded. His hand rested on the bar top, the fingers twitching one final time seeking to retrieve that masterly touch.

The clock on the wall ticked away the seconds. An ominous reminder of man's mortality. The unassailable fact that time on this earth is limited and can easily be cut short. Everybody was holding their breath, waiting on the gunman's call.

Wesco was enjoying the notoriety he had created. He was confident that the Reno Kid's three years of sedentary habits would have noticeably slowed his reactions. With due purpose, he delayed the moment of truth. The ugly smirk urged his opponent to lose his nerve. But Reno held firm. The delaying tactics had actually strengthened his resolve. Old habits had flooded back through his veins. His mindset had reverted to that of the ruthless bounty hunter of old.

'When you're ready, Doyle.' The terse retort was hissed out, removing the gunman's smug conceit. 'We don't want to keep these good folks waiting, do we?'

Somewhat deflated that his strategy had failed to pay dividends, Wesco Doyle's blotched visage twisted into an ugly grimace.

The coin rose into the thick air. Sunlight beaming in through the front window caught the spinning facets. Reaching its zenith, the twisting harbinger of doom began a flight towards destiny. Fate now hung in the balance. As if in slow motion the coin moved inexorably towards the point of no return.

Chhiiinnngg!

The sharp rattle as the coin touched ground echoed around the room. Both protagonists grabbed for their weapons. Each fired at almost the same moment. Two shots blending into one. A scream could be heard from behind the closed door of the back office. But nobody paid it any heed. Smoke belched from the two revolvers. An oil lamp behind Reno's head shattered into a myriad fragments.

But it was Doyle who clutched at his chest. A look of surprise, total and absolute, was etched across the startled visage. Too late the fact registered in his rapidly failing brain that he had sadly underestimated his opponent.

Then he slid to the floor. The Kid walked across and stood over the dying gunman, his own weapon trained on the guy's chest, just in case there was still any fight left in the shattered frame. But the oozing spread of scarlet across his shirt said otherwise.

'I judged you wrong, Reno . . .' Doyle gasped out. 'Guess a man . . . never does lose . . . that ability. . . .' His head dropped onto his chest; a harsh rasping in his throat told of only seconds remaining.

'I never meant to shoot your brother in the back, Wesco,' Reno assured his dying adversary, bending down. 'It was a mistake. He turned away.'

'Gee . . . I know that. . . . But a man has to try and . . . salvage some family pride. . . . And maybe I was secretly hoping to take over . . . where Leroy failed. . .' A gurgle meant to be a guffaw rumbled inside the heaving torso. More urgent gasps. One final lifting of the large head followed as Doyle's watery gaze settled on the Reno Kid. 'More fool me . . . eh? Maybe next time. . . .'

But there would be no second chance for Wesco Doyle.

The gunman slid over on to his face. One more death chalked up to the infamous bounty hunter known as the Reno Kid. The killer felt no sense of euphoria, no satisfaction. Indeed, he felt deflated by the whole sorry incident. Placing the revolver on the bar top he hurried to the back office.

Marcia had already left. Cole headed for the back door intending to follow and plead his case, but Flush Harry barred his way.

'Leave her be, Cole,' he cautioned although his voice held a note of warning as well. 'You've sunk your boats where Marcia is concerned. She don't want any more to do with you. And she meant it.'

'But you know that I wasn't given any choice, Harry. I had to face him down.' There were tears in his eyes knowing that the new life he had established in Maverick was falling apart.

The gambler led him back to a chair. He poured out a liberal shot of whiskey and handed it to his partner and best friend. 'Sure I do. And so does every man in this town. They'll all back your play.' He paused, not quite knowing how to voice his next announcement. 'But Marcia don't see it that way. She reckons you never really abandoned your old ways.'

'That ain't true!' Cole blurted out.

Donovan ignored the interruption. 'She figures that

killing Doyle is only the start. And she has a point, Cole. It's only a matter of time before the news gets out and other scum of his ilk drift down here to try their luck.' He was now thinking of his own standing in the community and what the arrival of numerous young guns eager for a shoot-out would mean for the town.

Cole stood up. 'I have to see her. To explain.'

'Too late for that,' Donovan insisted. 'She's taking Joey to stay with her mother over in Dragoon Wells. She gave me strict instructions to prevent any contact between the three of you.'

'So what are you saying, Harry?' It was now Cole Rickard's voice that had hardened as the grim reality of what he had set in motion struck home like a gun barrel over the head.

'I'm sorry, Cole. Looks like it's the end.' Donovan hurried on. 'You'll have to leave town, old buddy. That's another choice you have forfeited. Of course, I'll buy out your share of the business. But you can't stay here now.'

Cole Rickard gritted his teeth. He was now more angry than upset. 'A leopard never changes its spots. Is that it? My past reputation will never be forgotten until some young tearaway ends it permanently.'

The gambler shrugged. 'You said it, not me. I suggest you head home and pack your gear. I'll have the dough ready when you return.'

What Flush Harry had failed to divulge was that the arrival of Wesco Doyle had been his doing. Now that Doyle was dead, there was nobody left to divulge his fatal indiscretion. He was hugely thankful that the dead man had not revealed the source of his knowledge. And if the Reno Kid also left town, there was no reason for trouble to raise its ugly head in Maverick.

Nevertheless, the unpleasant occurrence had left him shaken and ashen-faced.

Luckily for Donovan, Cole was not thinking of how Doyle had discovered his whereabouts. He was too wrapped up in his own sorry predicament. After gathering up his meagre belongings, he returned to the Buckeye for the final farewell.

'Good luck to you, Cole,' the gambler said as they shook hands. 'Take care out there. And watch how you go.' The beads of sweat bubbling on his rotund face passed unnoticed by the woebegone bounty hunter.

So after three good years, it was *término*! There was no more to be said. Cole Rickard, now once again having to don the despised persona of the Reno Kid, pushed his ex-partner aside and left the saloon by the back door.

THREE

HAPPY JACK

The recollection of that fateful day in Maverick had left Cole morose and dejected.

Was he heading down a box canyon where the only way out was back the way he had come? Surely, after all this time, Marcia would have mellowed and would be prepared to at least talk it through. Try to see their schism from his point of view. Or was he only fooling himself? Would he never be able to shrug off the past except by booking that plot in the graveyard?

He had come this far. There was only one way to discover what destiny had in store for the Reno Kid. With a heavy heart he mounted up and nudged the sorrel back into motion. He could only hope and pray that his exhortations would pay dividends.

The narrow trail pursued a meandering course between clusters of orange sandstone. Wind-scoured buttes rose up on either side with clumps of juniper and greasewood scrabbling for life amidst the arid wilderness. After pushing over the rimrock, the trail began a lazy descent towards the sprawling plateau land below.

If his figuring was right, the town of Happy Jack ought to be just over that next range of foothills.

It was the following afternoon when the narrow deer track he had been following crested a low rise. Below, on the level plain, sat a tiny cluster of buildings. Reno's eyes lifted in surprise. Happy Jack was nought but a remote trading post. Mudlark Sullivan, the old prospector he had encountered while crossing the Mogollons, had led him to believe it was a place of some standing. Maybe it was just that to an old-timer used to living the solitary life in the wilderness.

The main log cabin was connected to another structure by a covered awning. It looked like a bunkhouse where travellers could stop over for the night. On the other side was a lodgepole enclosure holding a milk cow, a couple of dirty pigs and a few scrawny chickens.

The rider pushed down the gently shelving slope, cantering across the open spread of sagebrush. Drawing closer to the isolated settlement, it was clear that other travellers were inside. Three horses were tied up outside. Their heads hung down in the harsh noonday heat.

Happy Jack was named after Jackson Thorpe who had established the post some twenty years before. A toothy, good-natured grin had endeared him to miners and cowboys alike. It was a pack of renegade Apache bucks who had not appreciated the chatty proprietor's garrulous humour. Jack was found one day with a dozen arrows in his back. All that had been stolen was his stock of moonshine liquor and a couple of old flint-lock rifles.

Since then, owners of the trading post had been much less jovial. Yet the place still retained its contrary name. Perhaps to raise a smile in an otherwise unforgiving landscape. It had certainly worked for Cole Rickard. He was more than ready to avail himself of the facilities on offer.

But as he neared the lonely outpost, the usual studied vigilance once again took control. Always the cautious operator, Cole moved across to tether his own mount to a lone palo verde tree on the blind side of the main building. The drooping branches, still cloaked in their array of golden flowers, provided some welcome shade for the tired animal. Before entering the trading post, he filled a bucket with water from the trough and allowed his cayuse to slake its thirst.

Then he loosened the revolver in its holster. A man in his position could never be too careful. That was how he had managed to survived so long in such a precarious calling. With due care, he pushed open the heavy wooden door. Before entering he gave the interior a panoramic scan that took in everything at a glance.

Two men sat at a table, their attention focussed on plates of food. One was a Mexican. A wide heavily adorned sombrero oversaw the obligatory drooping moustache and flashing eyes. The latter now appraised the newcomer with a hint of the curious rather than any leaning towards animosity.

The other guy was older and of Anglo descent. Stout of girth as opposed to the Mexican's lithe build, his gaze was focussed wholly on the food, which he shovelled into a gaping maw with evident relish.

Satisfied they posed no threat, Cole gingerly took a step across the threshold.

'No need to be so jumpy, stranger,' said the man behind the counter. The proprietor poured a shot of whiskey and pushed it across the bar. 'Mosey on over here. First drink is on the house. I ain't got the same beaming grin as my predecessor, but that don't mean I can't make folks welcome at Happy Jack. The name's Amos Coolidge, but most folks call me Cowpat. Can't figure out why. But it don't matter none.'

The guy's square head with its circlet of dirty brown hair was a clear giveaway as to how he had acquired the derisory handle. Having the appearance of a dead polecat, it was a badly made wig. Cole suppressed a smile and the overwhelming desire to stare.

The moment quickly passed. Yet Cole still hung back. Three nags, two customers. So where was the third guy? Once again searching eyes flitted around the room, a cautious hand resting on the gun butt. Coolidge seemed genuine enough, but an innate caution born of an instinct for survival held him back.

'You sure are a nervous dude, ain't yuh?' snorted the proprietor.

Cole continued to scan the shadowy far recesses of the room as he replied, 'You ever heard the saying, "There's always free cheese in a mousetrap"?'

'Can't say that I have,' said the proprietor creasing up his mousey features in thought. Then the nickel dropped along with the hospitable beam.

'Well, heeding that snippet of finely honed piece of logic has kept me alive in a tough world.'

'That ees very good saying, *señor*,' the Mexican concurred with a judicious nod of approval. 'You are right to be *sospechoso*.' A wry smirk crossed the handsome profile while a finger jabbed at his chest. 'Fernando Estrela treat all *hombres* with same caution until he get to know them.'

Cole gave the poignant remark a justifiable bow of acknowledgement.

'Only trying to be friendly, is all,' grumbled the trader. 'You don't want a free drink? Ain't no skin off'n my nose.' Coolidge removed the glass and began pouring the contents back into the bottle. 'But there's no need to be—' He stopped in mid-flow. The beady eyes screwed up as he studied the newcomer more closely. 'Don't I know you from somewhere, mister?'

'Another bottle over here, Cowpat.' Mustang Charlie Bassett had suddenly discovered his own voice.

Cole now had a better look at him. Stout and rather bullish and sporting a broken nose, Bassett ignored the newcomer. The request emerged as a blurry gabble. Shreds of food clung to his beard as Bassett continued forking a large *tortilla española* into his mouth. The jasper clearly enjoyed filling his ample belly.

His summons for more alcoholic sustenance had temporarily interrupted Cowpat's line of thought. Grabbing a full bottle off the back shelf, the proprietor sauntered over and set it down on the table. 'Where's Frank gone?' he asked pointing to the abandoned plate opposite broken nose.

A twitch of the bullet head indicated the back door. 'Out back taking a leak.'

Cowpat nodded before returning to his side of the counter. Cole joined him, having satisfied himself that no skulduggery was afoot. The guy's own features were now much more plainly delineated.

'So what is it to be, stranger?' the trader asked. 'Most guys who call here welcome a free drink. There again, maybe you've heard good things about my woman's special *tortillas*. Each one freshly made. That it?' He called across to the guzzling diner seeking confirmation. 'You enjoying those on your plate, Mustang?'

A grunted response was accompanied by a nondescript shrug. Cowpat took that as a positive reaction. He was about to restate his inquiry when his gaze was again drawn to the angular profile of the newcomer.

'Get me a jug of buttermilk. My throat's burning up,' Cole croaked out.

The trader raised a bushy eyebrow at the unusual request then called out to his wife in the back room. 'One jug of milk out here, woman!'

'Travelling far?' The inquiry was merely to fill in time until the beverage arrived.

'Some.' Cole's reply was curt and non-committal. 'Got me some unfinished business to take care of in Maverick.'

But the garrulous proprietor was not listening. The strange hairpiece appeared to shift on its balding support as Cowpat snapped a thumb and finger together.

'I remember now,' evinced the animated trader, jabbing a finger at the newcomer. 'You're the Reno Kid. I was up in Denver when you brought in Black Dog Bowdrie. You came into the Occidental saloon for a drink after delivering the cuss to the marshal's office. I was chief bartender. That was one mean-eyed son-of-a-bitch you'd caught there. Guess he fetched a high bounty.'

Cole's back stiffened. This was the last thing he needed. Recognition this far south. He had not oper-ated in Arizona for more than four years.

At that moment Cowpat's Indian wife appeared with the jug of buttermilk. The Apache squaw known as Ponkasante had been sold to Amos Coolidge by her tribe the previous fall. No consent from the woman was sought by the tribal elders. No discussion instigated, except over the final bill of sale. Apache law had spoken and Ponkasante had to obey, or face death by stoning.

And so she was given over to a grim life as little more than a slave to the trader.

The squaw gave the lone traveller more than her usual surly regard. This man was different from the regular array of drifters who passed through Happy Jack. It was unusual for a white-eyes to order such a bev-erage. His bearing was alert, watchful and wary, but hinted of a deep sadness within. She stood a moment contemplating the torment that lay behind those doleful eyes.

The brief twinkling of introspection was abruptly curtailed.

'Back where you belong, woman,' rapped her husband. 'There's work to be done.'

The unintended interruption gave Cole time to think of a suitable response to Amos Coolidge's startling declaration. Pouring out a glass of the delicious beverage, Cole knocked it back in a single draught. His mouth crinkled into a half-smile as he wiped a hand across his mouth.

'Boy, that sure hit the spot and no mistake,' he sighed, pouring another glass. 'Much obliged, ma'am.'

Ponkasante returned the smile. It was her first such display since arriving at the trading post all those months before. A man had actually acknowledged her existence. Returning to her chores, the woman's step was much lighter. She would remember the hard-boiled yet gently considerate stranger for many moons to come. His solicitude would elicit a glow of hope in the dark days that lay ahead, a splash of colour into her life of menial drudgery.

But Cowpat was not to be sidetracked. 'What you doing in these parts then, Reno? I thought your baili-wick was up north in Colorado.'

Cole quickly shook his head. 'You got the wrong fella, mister. My name is Cole Rickard. And I ain't never been to Denver.'

This time it was Coolidge who shook his head along with the precarious rug perched thereon. 'Don't cotton to that notion. Amos Coolidge never forgets a face. I'm just like the elephant that never forgets –

'cept with me being a mite on the leaner side, of course.' He laughed at the witticism expecting the Kid to join in as confirmation of his claim.

'Well this time you're on the wrong trail, friend.' Cole's voice hardened as he held the other's gaze in a frosty grip. 'Like I just told you, the name is Cole Rickard. Now scarper and let me alone to enjoy my drink in peace.'

Cowpat shrugged then backed off. He could recognize the icy cut of a cold-eyed gunslinger from a hundred paces. Giving the newcomer a quizzical frown he moved across to join Fernando and Mustang Charlie.

Moments later they were joined by his partner.

'Could have sworn that guy was the Reno Kid,' Cowpat averred scratching his ear. He threw another surreptitious glance towards the milk drinker. 'In fact, I'm darn certain it's him. So why does he not want to be eyeballed?'

'I have never met thees *hombre* before, but he sure wears hees gun like he know how to use it.' The Mexican stuck a cheroot in his mouth and lit up.

The two other men looked at one another. Frank Quintel was a young punk who wore his own six-shooter low in a fancy tooled rig. On hearing the name of the legendary bounty hunter, his eyes lit up. Bassett, fifteen years his senior and far more circumspect, instantly perceived the gleam of fire in his partner's lurid smirk. He had seen it often enough before. And it spelled trouble.

'I reckon he's scared,' jeered the cocky braggart.

'Getting too old for gunplay.'

'Easy there, Frank,' Bassett cautioned laying a restrictive hand on the hothead's arm. 'The boss don't want no trouble. Remember what we're here for.'

'Charlie ees right, *muchacho*. It not good to draw attention to good selves.'

The three men were awaiting the arrival of Jeb Quintel; the boss of the notorious outlaw gang known as the Shadow Riders was also the elder brother of Frank Quintel. They were intending to rob the wagon carrying the monthly army payroll to Fort Defiance. Cowpat always received a cut for providing the gang with a hangout.

Jeb had sent the trio on ahead to brief Cowpat while he sussed out the bank in Globe for their next job. The rest of the gang were headed for Pima Pass where the stage was expected around noon in three days' time. They would camp out there until the boss and his three associates joined them.

'You hear me, boy?' pressed Mustang. 'Getting caught up in some showdown could spoil Jeb's plan.'

But Frank was not listening. He brushed off his buddies' caution with a surly grimace. 'You pair of boobies might be afraid of this dude, but I sure ain't. My betting is the yeller-belly don't want us knowing the truth cos he's lost his nerve. That'll give me the edge to take him out.'

'Don't be such a durned fool,' urged a suddenly much irritated Charlie Bassett. 'Guys like that eat young gunnies for breakfast. Jeb asked me to tag along to keep you out of trouble. Now heed my advice and let the guy drink his milk in peace.'

Such a churlish rebuke would have received Quintel's full ire had he not been so eager to challenge the renowned bounty hunter. But the young pretender was past any sort of dissuasion, no matter how vigorously espoused. All he could see was his name being spoken of in awe as the gunslinger who beat the Reno Kid to the draw.

Settling his rig comfortably, Frank Quintel rose from his seat and ambled over to the counter. The cracked smile held no levity. It was cold as a mountain stream. Here was an easy way to gain the reputation he had always craved. Move out of the shadow of his older brother. Cold eyes glittered at the thought of becoming famous throughout the Southwest.

'Over here, Cowpat,' he rasped. 'Give me a shot of whiskey. I need a real drink.'

The trader did as bid then hissed out a muted warning. 'I don't want no trouble in here. You listening to me, Frank?'

But the kid ignored him, knocking the drink back in a single gulp. He slammed the glass down on the counter hoping to jerk a reaction from the other man. Cole remained immune to the intended provocation.

'Never figured a tough big shot like the Reno Kid would stoop to drinking baby juice.' His reedy voice was laced with acrimony. 'Guess that rep of your'n was all make-believe after all. You ain't no more than a mama's boy.'

Cole looked straight ahead ignoring the rancid jibe. The last thing he wanted was more trouble now that he was so close to his goal. He lifted the glass and slowly imbibed the white liquid.

Yet deep down, he was seething. Not on account of the blatant insult. That was like water off a duck's back. Cole knew exactly where this dilemma was heading. There was to be no easy way out. This young tough was intent on a showdown. And nothing was going to stay his hand.

A wolfhound raised its head over by the fireplace. The dog's low growl cut through the atmosphere like butter. Instinctively sensing the sudden tension in the room, its fur stood on end.

Again, a sweating Cowpat tried appealing to reason. 'No need for this, Frank,' he nervously implored the hothead. 'Reno here was just leaving. Ain't that so, Kid?'

Both men were deaf to the panic-stricken entreaty. Cole knew that the escalating confrontation had shuffled beyond any possibility of a climb-down by either party. Yet still he tried.

'Can't you corral this hot-headed greenhorn, fella? How am I supposed to enjoy my drink with him breathing down my neck?' Cole couldn't help himself, he was so annoyed. The entreaty was to Mustang Charlie, clearly the more mature of the trio.

But it was Fernando who spoke up. 'Now it has come down to thees, *señor*, I Fernando Estrela, am more than a leetle intrigued to see eef the great Reno Kid ees all they say he ees.' The Mexican casually pursed his lips and pushed a perfect smoke ring into the fetid air.

Rather than cooling the heated exchange, the

greaser's remark had only inflamed the situation. Charlie merely shrugged his shoulders. He turned aside, washing his hands of the whole fiasco, merely muttering, 'Jeb ain't gonna like it.'

Frank snarled out a rabid epithet, his pudgy face glistening with sweat. The kid's right hand flexed above the gun butt of a bone-handled Colt Frontier. 'Nobody speaks to me like that, old man,' he barked out. Legs akimbo and hunkering down, he adopted the hunched stance of a gunslick who was beyond the pale. 'Fernando is right. Let's see how good you really are. Now if'n your backbone ain't filled with that cow slop, make your play.'

Cole levered himself off the counter. He fastened a probing eye on to the challenger. His usual ploy in such situations was always to let his antagonist draw first. Intuition and experience had taught him the skill of studying a man's body language. And it never varied. A slight widening of the eyes, a lift of the shoulder.

And so it was with Frank Quintel. The impatience of youth took its toll, the kid drawing first. His gun rose, hammer snapping back ready to deliver its lethal charge. The index finger tightened on the trigger. But it never managed the final hallelujah.

Cole's revolver bucked once only. It was enough. The gun appeared to have jumped into his right hand.

A plume of red blossomed on Frank's shirt. He looked down in shock. This was not how it should have been. Then his punctured body lurched backwards, tumbling over a chair. A final twitch of muscles and he lay still.

The smoking gun immediately swung to cover Mustang Charlie and the Mexican. Both outlaws raised their arms.

'Don't shoot, Reno. I ain't got no wish to stoke up the fiery furnace,' Bassett professed with vigour. 'Frank sure had it coming to him. But Jeb Quintel won't be so forgiving. And he's due here within the hour.'

In his mind's eye, Charlie could see the payroll snatch continuing on its merry way unimpeded. The leader of the Shadow Riders would want revenge before any more jobs were pulled. Frank was his only family. Then another thought entered his head. This would give Punk Adler the chance to muscle in and stir things up with the rest of the gang. But the steady six-shooter pointing at his belly quickly pushed the notion from his head.

Cole likewise knew that he would need to hit the trail and disappear into the wilds of Arizona before the gang boss could organize any pursuit. He resolutely cursed his bad luck in running into yet another reckless hotspur. But that was what his sorry life had become. One gunfight after another. Would it never end? Maybe there really was no way back.

Cole grabbed a fistful of jerked beef sticks along with the milk jug as he backed out of the trading post. Happy Jack's had suddenly lost any humour it had hoped to imbue in its most recent visitor. Downing the rest of the milk, he tossed the jug aside and mounted up. A wary eye was kept locked onto the windows of the post to ensure none of the occupants tried to delay his departure.

No sign of a gun barrel appeared as he spurred away. But he knew that Jeb Quintel was due in from his visit to Globe soon. As luck would have it, their paths were unlikely to cross, although the vengeful brother of Frank Quintel in company with Mustang Charlie and the greaser would not waste any time in dogging his trail.

There was only one way to deal with such a pursuit.

FOUR

CAST AFOOT

Cole eventually found a suitable cluster of boulders from which to set up an ambush. He concealed the sorrel in a clump of cottonwoods then clambered up onto the ledge overlooking the open trail. There, he settled down to await his pursuers. The beef jerky provided some much needed sustenance.

Ensconced beneath a convenient rocky overhang sheltered from the harsh sun, he had no idea how long his vigil would last. Would Quintel come straight after him? Or would he decide to stay over at Happy Jack and wait until the following day? One thing was beyond question: if Mustang Charlie's assertion was correct, follow he surely would to enact justice for his slain brother.

Had Cole still been an active bounty hunter he would have sought to take the guy in. But those days were now in his past. At least, that was his sincere hope.

Trouble in the disreputable form of the Devil unfortunately had a bad habit of popping up to burst your bubble.

The shooting of Frank Quintel was a melancholic example of the horned demon's conniving tactics.

His thoughts returned to the task in hand. All he could do now was to wait it out. He prayed that the inevitable confrontation would be sooner rather than later.

His morbid anticipation was to be rewarded. Two hours after establishing himself on the shelf of rock, the silence was broken by a dull yet regular thud of hoof beats. And they were coming from the direction of Happy Jack. Cole tossed away the half-eaten stick of jerky and crawled to edge of the shelf.

Rifle at the ready, he removed his hat and peered over the lip. The open plain provided an unrestricted vista for miles. The rising plume of yellow dust was about half a mile back. He could make out three riders. It had to be Jeb Quintel and his two sidekicks. Within minutes they were approaching the ambush site. Cole gave a nod of satisfaction on recognizing the distinctively brutish features of Broken Nose.

He had never laid eyes on the elder Quintel before. However, his reputation, if not the name, as an effective outlaw leader of the Shadow Riders was well known. So was the knife scar he carried above his left eye. A white slash in contrast to the black brow opposite gave him a wolfish appearance. The gang had intimidated the territory for two years without capture, disappearing after each caper like shadows in the night.

Hence the name allotted by Sheriff Grant Souther of Prescott.

The guy sat tall in the saddle and carried himself with a confident ease. Cole knew he would have to be extra vigilant when handling the outlaw boss.

He waited until the trio were no more than fifty yards from the shelf before he despatched two bullets. Each ploughed into the hard-packed ground immediately ahead of the riders. Gouts of sand spurted into the air, startling the horses. The animals reared up on their hind legs and stumbled to a halt. Before the men could react, Cole was on his feet, the rifle at his shoulder.

'Hold it right there!'

The blunt order was measured and restrained, yet issued in a terse threat that could not be ignored. He had no wish to have any more deaths on his conscience. In the old days he would not have hesitated in blasting these critters out of their saddles. But his brash life as a ruthless manhunter and firebrand was over. Enough killing had been done to last him a half dozen lifetimes.

Indeed, he shivered at the notion that such a lifestyle had been his career of choice. Any terminal gunplay now would only be as a last resort. Earlier on this very day he had been forced into yet another fatal showdown; Frank Quintel had given him no room for manoeuvre. But when he was offered an alternative, it had to be to give his adversaries an even break. This was such a moment.

His aim now was merely to prevent these jaspers

from following him. And he knew just how that could be achieved without blood being spilled. It was now their choice to determine whether they would see another sunrise.

'OK, boys!' he hollered making sure to keep the pursuers covered. 'Raise your hands and step down. Any false moves and this long gun will finish the argument permanently.'

Quintel snarled. But the outlaw knew better than to resist. The men slid off their mounts.

'And keep them mitts high and wide.'

Maintaining his watch on the captives, Cole scuttled down from his lofty perch. Warily, he approached the three men. It was Quintel who spoke first.

'You could have prevented it being a killing shot, Reno,' came the rasping accusation. He was referring to his deceased kin.

'I wasn't given any choice,' responded Cole firmly.

Quintel's reaction was to be expected. A disdainful snort said it all. 'There's always a choice. You went for the wrong one. Frank was only a young kid. Sure, he was a tearaway. But he was my brother. I ain't about to forget that in a hurry. You best watch your back from now on.'

'A backshooter, is that it, Quintel?' Cole hawked a wad of chewing tobacco at the outlaw's feet. 'I might have known a lowlife of your ilk couldn't face a man down.'

Quintel's face turned a darker shade of purple. He was almost tempted to go for his gun. It was Mustang's restraining hand that prevented an early visit from the

Reaper. 'Hold up, Jeb. He's only trying to goad you.'

'You'd do well to heed your buddy, mister,' advised Cole. 'He's got some sense. He'll also tell you that Frank knew what he was about.' Cole was vainly hoping to persuade the incensed outlaw to accept his claim that the shooting was unavoidable. It was a vain hope, but still he tried. 'All these young guns are the same. He wanted to be the one who bested the Reno Kid. It was self-defence. Frank drew first.'

Cole looked to the other man for confirmation. Mustang shrugged. It was not his call. And the Shadow leader was not about to heed any excuses. 'Frank stood no chance against a gunslick of your calibre. It was pure murder. Make no mistake, mister, I'm gonna seek you out and do the job properly. Then it'll be Jeb Quintel who can strutt his stuff. *I'll* be the jasper who outgunned the Reno Kid.'

'Well it ain't gonna be anytime soon.' Cole was becoming tired of the aimless chitchat. 'Enough of this jaw-jabbering. Now shuck them irons, pronto.'

Quintel ran his tongue along the length of his thin lips.

Cole recognized the signs. Yet another hint that a sly rat was working out the odds of beating his captor to the draw. Always alert for the cunning ploys practised by most experienced gunmen, he studied Jeb Quintel's reactions. He was no brazen tenderfoot like his brother and would require extra care.

Instead of untying his leg thongs, the outlaw hooked his thumbs into the gunbelt. A sigh of resignation hissed from the cruel mouth as if to admit he had been thwarted by a better man. To Cole's experienced eye it was a sure sign of an imminent challenge.

'Don't try it, mister.' Cole's voiced had changed to a hard, brittle snap. He lifted the rifle meaningfully. 'Only a mug would figure the Reno Kid wasn't clued up on all the sneaky tricks critters like you go for.' An ugly leer challenged Jeb Quintel to make his move. The outlaw was left in no doubt that a dose of lead poisoning from Doctor Death would be his sure-fire remedy for such a reckless deed. 'Now, all you jerks, ditch them belts.'

Quintel scowled. But he was no fool. He knew it was going to take more than a one-to-one contest to crack this nut. The three men slowly did as ordered. The chance of getting the better of the renowned bounty hunter had passed them by.

'Now it's the turn of your boots and socks.' The mirthless smirk remained pasted onto the gunfighter's leathery features. His order found the men protesting vigorously. Cole allowed them to voice their complaints without interruption.

'You can't cast us afoot in this godforsaken wilderness,' Quintel griped. 'It ain't human. Our feet'll be cut to ribbons without socks.'

'Have a heart, Mister Reno,' pleaded Mustang trying to ingratiate himself. 'We've learned our lesson. You won't get no more trouble from us. Ain't that right, Jeb?'

The gang boss was forced to swallow his pride. 'Guess I was trying to overreach myself. And Frank always was a knuckleheaded mule. How are we gonna

49

survive out here without boots?'

All the fight appeared to have drained out of the hard-nosed villain. But Cole was not moved by the feeble petitions. He had heard all these excuses many times before. None of it washed with him.

'I won't tell you again. Dump the footwear. All of it.'

His brusque mandate was sharp and to the point. And Quintel knew that Reno would have no compunction in carrying out the threat. Bullets would fly should more disputes be forthcoming. A series of suppressed grunts found the three wretched gunmen barefoot and unarmed.

'Now get to walking,' Cole snarled. 'You should make it back to Happy Jack in maybe three days . . . if'n you're lucky and don't step on no rattlers or scorpions. And then there's the gila monsters. Those fellas just don't know when to let go once they grab a hold of yuh. It sure would be a pity for that to happen. Now get moving!'

A flick of the rifle urged the glowering barefooted outlaws to set off back the way they had come.

'I'll get even with you, Reno, if'n it's the last thing I do,' growled Quintel. 'And don't think for a minute that showing us mercy will save you.' But it was an impotent throwaway lacking any teeth.

'Could be you're right, Quintel,' Cole tossed back. 'Maybe I have been too darned soft.' He loosed off a couple of slugs that found the three crooks dancing a merry jig. A hearty guffawing from their tormentor jarred in Quintel's ears. 'Watch where you put them feet, boys,' the chuckling subjugator shouted.

'Tarantulas are also known to inhabit these hills. And their bite ain't to be relished neither. Enjoy the walk.'

The three downcast ruffians immediately abandoned their simmering rancour and threw all their attention into avoiding any such denizens that might increase their suffering. Cole waited until they were well out of sight before continuing with his own journey south.

Again his brow furrowed in thought. Quintel and his boys were forgotten as he drew ever closer to his ultimate goal.

FIVE

LUCK OF THE DEVIL

For the first hour after being cast afoot, the sole aim of the owlhoots was to avoid any sharp protrusions. Apart from numerous grunts and curses when hidden snares dug into their soft skin, silence reigned. Fernando led the way. As a poverty-stricken child brought up in the slums of Nogales, shoes were a luxury only worn on Sundays. As a result his feet were tough as old leather.

Jeb and Mustang soon had to rest up. Already their feet were bleeding.

'We can't go on like this,' the older man mumbled. Removing his bandanna, he gently dabbed at the torn skin. 'What we gonna do, Jeb?'

The whinging voice held a note of panic that the gang boss was not slow in denigrating to conceal his own burgeoning fears. 'Cut your grousing, Mustang.

We'll get out of this soon enough.' He did not elaborate. Nor did Bassett. A far more serious issue suddenly occurred to the old bronc-buster.

'What we gonna do for water out here?' He peered around mournfully.

Quintel silently cursed his stupidity. The hollow gaze that blankly scanned the arid terrain held no answer to such a basic problem. So intent had all three been on avoiding any mishaps, they had overlooked that most vital of elements.

It was Fernando who came to the rescue. He had walked on ahead and come upon a clump of beavertail cacti. Hacking off the sharp spines with a rock, he broke open one of the large green plates. Inside was a stringy mush. After peeling away the hard outer shell, he sucked on the damp flesh. It tasted bitter, but was better than nothing and would keep them going until they reached Happy Jack.

'Over this way, *muchachos*,' he called out. 'Here lies our salvation.' The other two hobbled over to join him. 'Do not expect vintage champagne. But cactus *agua* will stop our bodies from drying up.'

Seeing their buddy sucking on the green plate, Quintel and the ex-bronc-peeler immediately fell upon them. True, the moisture within tasted foul. But beggars can't be choosers, as the saying goes.

They were now able to fully appreciate the manner in which these bizarre desert dwellers were able to thrive and produce such a prized tonic. Both men promised themselves that when they escaped this torment, never again would either take the fruits of the desert for granted. With their thirst temporarily slaked, the three castaways continued their shambling journey. The pace slowed to little more than a stumbling plod. Bassett was getting on Quintel's nerves with his constant bleating. He gritted his teeth and closed his mind to the griping. Head down, he ploughed on.

The Mexican had again wandered ahead. Suddenly, another buoyant summons edged with hope found the two sorry *gringos* scurrying as best they could round to the far side of a rock stack. There they found Fernando beside the weathered bones of a long abandoned wagon. Much of it was buried in a sand drift. But it was the canvas cover the Mexican was ripping apart with a rusty knife that caught their attention.

As well as the knife, there was also an array of ragged clothing.

'Eh, boys,' he exclaimed gleefully. 'We are een luck again, *si?* With these things we make our own footwear.'

An hour later, they were back on the trail, and making better progress. The makeshift footwear was cumbersome, but offered some much appreciated protection. The mood suddenly lightened. Jeb Quintel was able to further add to the upbeat raising of spirits with a surprise announcement.

A couple of miles further on, he signalled a halt beside a large organ pipe cactus.

Bassett slumped to the ground. 'I'm plum tuckered out,' he groaned. 'You fellas go on. Come back for me when you reach Happy Jack.'

'No need for that, Mustang,' breezed a grinning Jeb

Quintel. 'Ain't much further now.' Bassett gave him a lop-sided grimace of puzzlement.

'How you figure that?' asked the equally baffled Mexican.

Quintel was enjoying the subterfuge. 'This is where we swing off the trail, boys,' he declared with a sly grin.

'But this ees not thee way to Happy Jack,' evinced the puzzled Fernando. 'Why you go thees way, *patrón*?'

'Over the other side of that ridge is a ranch where we can get some fresh mounts.' Quintel pointed to a notch in the rocky skyline ahead. Winding between clumps of sagebrush and the now much revered beavertails, the track headed straight towards it.

'How you know thees?' asked Fernando.

'It was afore I met up with you, boys,' he said. 'I was running with a gang of roughriders on the border with Utah in Monument Valley. We used to come out the canyons to hold up passing stagecoaches. Trouble was, we got to be too darned cocky. Kept operating the same plan of attack. That was our downfall.'

'One day we tried it on with another coach at the same spot. But this time it was filled with bluecoats. Half the gang were cut down or captured. Me and a guy called Montana Jaxx were the only ones to escape unscathed. We split up. I headed south. Jaxx reckoned to have salted enough away to buy a piece of land in California. I ain't heard from him since. So I figure he must have made it and settled down.'

Quintel scratched his head at the recollection. 'Never stick to the same routine. That's my advice to you boys. And I've followed it ever since. Those army jaspers had us sussed out. We didn't stand a chance.'

'You never mentioned this before, boss,' Mustang interrupted. 'I always reckoned you were a Nevada guy.'

'It don't always pay for a man to advertise his past,' cautioned the outlaw, tapping his nose with meaning. 'Mouthing off too much has a habit of biting you on the ass.'

'That ees wise thinking, *patron*. So how you come across thees ranch?' Fernando was eager to hear the finale seeing as it coincided with their current circumstances.

'I was heading south aiming to cross into Mexico.' Quintel was getting back into his stride. Hawking a sly wink at his Mexican buddy, he continued, 'Those *señoritas* down Sonora way sure know how to look after a guy, don't you think, Fern?'

The Mexican sighed. His eyes glazed over. 'You are indeed right there, *patrón*.'

'So what happened?' pressed Mustang, also eager to hear the rest of the story.

'I had a pesky suspicion that some dude was on my tail.' Red pokers glinted in Quintel's eyes. He spat on the ground. 'Might even have been that skunk Reno. Anyway, my cayuse was flagging badly. I needed a new one, and quick. Hoping to throw him off the scent, I turned off here. And just by chance, I came across this horse ranch.'

'The one over yonder?' Charlie pointed to the approaching ridgeline.

'One and the same. There was nobody about apart

from a corral full of ready-made broncs. I just grabbed the nearest one, saddled up and left mine.' He shrugged as if this was the most natural thing in the world. 'After all, fellas, don't they say that fair exchange is no robbery?'

The adage brought roars of laughter from his two associates. 'You sure are right there, boss,' agreed Charlie.

'Only trouble was, the owner didn't cotton to my generosity.' Gaping mouths greeted this sudden change in fortune. They hung on Quintel's every word, silently urging him to reach the conclusion. 'He came out the cabin at the moment I was mounting up, a gun in his hand. The varmint must have spotted the exchange.'

'What happened? Did he shoot you?' exclaimed Charlie.

'Still here, ain't I? But that poor dupe is strumming with the angels.' He crossed himself in mock acknowledgement of the wrangler's demise.

Following these strange revelations from their leader, the three footsloggers made a left along the thin track. It had been stamped out by a family of coyotes. They soon passed the skeleton of a dead antelope, its bleached bones now all that remained. With Fernando's arm around the hobbling Bassett, they pressed on towards the notch on the horizon.

Around late afternoon, they staggered up the final rise and over the lip. And there below, a verdant sward opened up with the all-important horse ranch at its heart.

The three men slumped to the ground gasping for breath. It had been a tiring trudge, even with their supply of beavertail plates and the makeshift footwear. Bassett lay on his back sucking in air.

Quintel heaved a sigh of relief that the ranch was still operating as such. And judging by the activity taking place, it was a thriving concern.

'We sure are in luck, boys,' he averred with gusto. 'It looks like they're doing good business down there.'

Mustang Charlie soon recovered from the arduous trek knowing they had reached what appeared to be their salvation. He was especially enthralled by the equine venture. Much of his life before taking to the owlhooter trail was on such enterprises. His practised gaze followed the skilled endeavour of the lone bronc-peeler to bend the wild horse to his will.

'Those guys can earn good money at this business,' he declared. 'A top hand can tame eight broncs a day earning himself five bucks a head. But it's tough work.'

'That sure ees *bueno dinero*,' maintained Fernando, impressed. 'Why you stop?'

Charlie stretched his tired limbs and creaking bones. 'Busting nags is apt to age a fella before his time. It's gruelling work. And I got the bruises, sprains and badly set bones to prove it.' He stretched his stiff shoulders. 'Mustangs ain't the only things that get busted.'

They were studying the action down below. It was a mesmerizing sight to behold the skilled bronc man at work. Charlie avidly filled them in with a detailed resumé of the wrangling task being enacted.

As one newly tamed cayuse was released into the holding pen another bounded into the fenced stockade. The bay gelding hammered around the enclosure trying to find a way out. The buster's first job was to throw a rope around its neck and lash it to a snubbing post. Gingerly, whispering sweet nothings, he slipped a hackamore bridle over the shaking head.

Bridled and hobbled but still full of fight, the toughest job was then to blanket and saddle the recalcitrant animal. The battle between man and beast can be a salutary lesson for both parties. Much as they wanted to cheer the guy on, the watchers were obliged to curb their passionate enthusiasm. Noise from the ridge could carry on the light desert zephyrs that scurried hither and thither up here.

Their breath was held in check as the rider failed in his first attempt to mount up. He would have been trampled underfoot by the stomping shoeless hoofs had he not jumped aside in the nick of time.

Approaching from a different angle, he used a slicker to divert the animal's attention long enough to successfully complete the intricate manoeuvre.

'That a boy,' hissed Charlie, slamming a bunched fist into the ground. 'You have him now. Get that cinch tightened pronto!'

The bronc-peeler seemed to hear the advice and instantly did as the old roustabout suggested. Charlie smiled. The horse began tossing and bucking, desperate to remove the irksome hindrance.

The buster was dragged around the stockade like a rag doll. Only by tugging and hauling on the rope was he able to maintain his footing. At the same time he drew closer to the crazed beast until he was near enough to grab the bay's ears. Squeezing hard, the animal whinnied. But the sudden pain was enough to distract the gelding, thus allowing the guy to swing aboard.

Now it was a question of teaching the cayuse the art of obedience. Gut-jarring hell broke out as the skittish gelding desperately tried to unseat the alien invader. Its back arched to an acute angle. But the man hung on. High above the mesmeric performance, the excited yells of glee from the buster could be clearly heard. Charlie Bassett almost joined in the frenetic cheering. Just in time he held back.

Clinging on to a short halter with his left hand, the buster began hazing the animal with the slicker. That and the judicious use of a quirt wrapped around his wrist were the principle means of persuasion as man and beast battled for supremacy. But there was only ever going to be one winner.

The man then rode the animal around the stockade, hauling up and dismounting on numerous occasions until he was satisfied the bay had gotten the message as to who was boss. As the tamed mount became used to its new master, soft words were spoken to show there were no hard feelings. And so another bronco was tamed.

The peeler wandered across to a water trough and removed his hat. Untying his necker, he dipped it into the scummy liquid. Without squeezing out the moisture, he dragged the cloth across his sweat-smeared face and neck. Arms stretched wide to ease the stiffness in his strained muscles.

'That surely was a fine sight,' Fernando concurred before adding a proviso. 'But no amount of dinero would persuade good self to engage in such work. It is now clear as fresh water, amigo, why you chose a life outside thee law.'

'We'll camp up here tonight,' said Quintel, 'and move down at daybreak to make our choice before those jaspers are awake.'

Mustang Charlie dragged his admiring thoughts away from the nostalgic sight below. All the excitement attached to the age-old contest betwixt man and beast was reflected in his wistful gaze. Having watched the scintillating performance, Charlie's eyes misted over as evocative thoughts of a past long since confined to history washed over him.

But that's all it was – an evocative longing for a way of life that had, in truth, only brought him aches and pains by the bucket load. And much as he had insisted that good money could be made by the top hands, there was no way such a brutal way of earning a crust could be sustained. Carry on like those guys below and he would have ended up kicked to death, or a helpless cripple. That notion was enough to persuade him that the right decision had been made.

You never clapped eyes on a bronc-peeler over the age of thirty. Most had either been forced to retire, or gone the way of Charlie Bassett.

The nostalgic yearning cast aside, the one-time buster took heed of the boss's take on the proceedings.

And he was not impressed.

Making camp up here was not a good idea. Bassett was the only member of the Shadow Riders who had the nerve to voice his dissention. Age, and his having ridden with Quintel for more than two years, had given him a certain degree of authority. The gang leader heeded his advice.

So it was that the old bronc-rider now aired his views.

Yet even he always chose to be prudent and circumspect in any suggestions he made that did not concur with those of Jeb Quintel. Like all arrogant jaspers who led from the front, the guy balked against his decisions being brought into question. But these were unusual, if not desperate circumstances that the three outlaws now found themselves in.

'I was thinking, boss, that maybe staying up here all night ain't such a good idea.'

He paused, holding his breath, and waited for Quintel to listen, or blow his top.

The gang boss turned towards his associate. His face was blank, ambiguous. It had always been Jeb Quintel's policy to heed any suggestions made by his owlhooter associates. There were times, though, when under stress, or more likely the influence of the demon drink, that he shunned any dissention. Hence Bassett's reticence.

The response was measured and acquiescent. 'You gotten a better plan, Charlie, then let's hear it.'

'There's a couple of hours' daylight left,' Bassett remarked. 'The rider down there will be calling it quits soon. I figure there are maybe just two guys in the outfit. The other one has likely finished early to rustle up some chow.' He pointed to a twist of smoke rising from the stack of the cabin. 'Looks like he's stoking up already.'

As if on cue, a man emerged from the cabin and began hammering on an iron ring. The buster lifted an arm in acknowledgement.

He went on to explain the scheme he had in mind.

'So what d'yuh figure, boss?'

Quintel hummed and hawed to himself as he tossed over the various ramifications involved with what Bassett had outlined. Both men waited. It was Fernando who spoke first. 'Ees good plan, *amigo*. Although why good self to go down first?'

Charlie was ready for that objection. 'That's cos I might know some of those dudes. We bronc men travel around and get to know each other. The last thing we need is an extra burr to complicate matters. And another thing. My face is on that wanted dodger we saw pinned up outside of Snowflake.'

'I agree,' Quintel concurred. 'It's a good plan. Well done, Charlie. That ain't just an ugly mush a-sitting on your shoulders.' It was a back-handed compliment much appreciated by the old buster. 'So this is how we'll carry it through.'

SIX

HORSING AROUND

The Mexican was instructed to wait on the ridge until the others were in position.

Quintel led the way down the slope. It was a painful descent through a tangle of mesquite and thorn that had the two men grimacing as the rough ground tormented their lacerated feet. It seemed like half a lifetime before they reached the easier flat terrain. Keeping to the cover of the corral fence, they sidled up to the rear of the barn. Being on the blind side of the log cabin prevented them being spotted by the busters.

Silent as wraiths, the two outlaws entered through the rear door of the barn and slipped inside. A row of stalls occupied by horses lined both sides. The freshly disciplined animals ignored the newcomers, continuing to munch on their feed bags.

It was clearly chow-time all round.

The nearest was a fine Appaloosa stallion that

Quintel immediately singled out for himself. 'Seems like you were right, Charlie,' he praised. 'Now all we have to do is wait on Fernando playing his part.'

He hobbled back to a corner of the barn and signalled to the Mexican through a window that they were in position. A raised arm was acknowledged from the ridge.

While they were waiting, Bassett's gazed focussed on the line of horse tack hanging on the wall. Lined up neatly was every kind of metal bit including spade, ring and curb, all well polished with no evident rust. Alongside were headstalls – the California, split and ever-popular hackamore, all in pristine condition as would be expected from a professionally efficient outfit as this clearly was.

As always, to a guy who had made his living with horses, it was the saddles that were of particular interest. One especially had caught his discerning eye. Not on account of its style – it was a standard Denver model – but this one had carvings on its cantle and rear skirt that he recognized.

Mustang Charlie frowned in concentration. Now where had he seen this saddle before? Unlike a wild bronc, a good saddle took much longer to break in. But once achieved to a rider's satisfaction, it was rarely changed. Horses came and went. But a good saddle was for life, or until it fell apart.

He was given no further time to cogitate on the baffling puzzle.

'On guard, Charlie,' Quintel whispered. 'Fernando has arrived.'

Fifteen minutes had passed when Estrela was seen approaching the log cabin from the front. The Mexican bandit's nerves were stretched tight as banjo strings. It took the greatest effort to espouse the casual demeanour of an innocent traveller in need of help. The forced smile glued to his visage was flat and cold.

He paused outside the cabin, drawing breath before calling out.

'*Hola, señors*! Anybody at home?'

Moments later the plank door opened a fraction and a gun barrel poked out. 'Who's there and what d'yuh want?' The gruff voice was laced with suspicion.

'My wagon has broken axle down thee trail. You help fix, *por favour, señor*? I haff money to pay.' He stepped forward.

'Hold it right there if'n you don't want a gutful of lead. How do I know you ain't some hoss thief?'

The blunt-edged challenge was immediately answered by the Mexican holding up his arms. 'Would I give warning if such were thee case? See, *señor*, I have no weapon. How can one lone *hombre* do you any harm?'

The bronc-peeler was still not convinced. Horse thieves were a constant hazard in this business. And nobody was above suspicion, especially a greaser. 'So why ain't you wearing any boots?' The query was spat out.

'*Caballos* attack me, which ees why I walk here for over two hours. Boots old. They split and fall apart.' The woebegone expression was no veil of deception. His feet really were sore.

66

A grunt followed as the speaker turned to discuss the matter with his sidekick inside the cabin. 'OK, guess you're on the level.'

The door opened wider and a bow-legged jasper stepped out. He was on the short side but held the Loomis shotgun with confidence. Fernando was not about to buck such a lethal deterrent.

'But I ain't taking no chances,' the man rasped. 'We had some thievin' varmints try their luck only last month. They're occupying unhallowed land over yonder. You go first. Over to the barn. But try any sly moves and you get both barrels. Now move!' He jerked the gun, urging the Mexican to about face.

'*Sí, sí, señor.* I no pull any tricks.'

Fernando's crafty smirk was hidden from the buster who was following behind. The scheme hatched by Mustang Charlie was going according to plan. The ex-buster had said that the newly broken horses would be housed inside the building. Clearly he was right.

Wild untamed cayuses could now be seen behind the buildings. They were securely caged in a strong pitch-pole corral. Such wild creatures would have kicked the plank structure to matchwood in no time. Newly tamed broncs were also kept separate to get them used to wearing a full saddle rig.

Inside the barn, the outlaw boss positioned himself and his sidekick on either side of the main door. 'You club him down with that jackpole soon as he comes through the door,' Quintel hissed, his voice a tremulous croak as the tension mounted. 'I'll cover you with this pitchfork.' The deadly prongs glinted in the sun-

67

light beaming in through the window.

Mustang gripped the heavy wooden implement tightly.

The muffled sound of footsteps heralded the imminent arrival of their quarry. A brisk nod between the ambushers and the door was pushed open. Fernando moved inside and quickly stepped to one side. The buster followed but his eyes took some seconds to accustom themselves to the dark interior.

That was the moment Charlie Bassett stepped out from behind the door and cracked him over the head. The dull thud echoed round the stark interior of the barn. The man went down like a sack of flour. He was out for the count. The door creaked shut on rusty hinges. Inside their stalls, the tamed horses continued with their repast, unaware of the violent action taking place in their midst.

'The other guy will soon come out the cabin when his buddy fails to appear,' muttered Bassett.

Quintel nodded. He peered down at the guy on the floor. Satisfied that he was out of action, the gang boss grabbed up the shotgun and moved across to a window overlooking the cabin some fifty yards distant. Unlike a rifle, these weapons were only effective at short range. 'All I need is for him to move closer. This beauty will do the rest.' He stroked the long gun's shiny rosewood stock.

Mustang stared down at the man lying on the ground. His eyes rolled, a shiver of dread filling his whole being. Now he knew where he had seen that saddle before. This guy was Ike Crawley, his old partner.

And he, Charlie Bassett had laid him out cold. Shock stunned the Mustang Man, his muscles cramping up. It had been an instinctive reaction to chop down Ike Crawley that he now deeply regretted. Previously, his attitude had been detached. Suddenly it had become personal. The guy had been a friend as well as a colleague. They had busted broncs together for two seasons before Charlie quit.

This meant that the other guy in the cabin had to be his son, Will.

How could he go through with this any longer? It wasn't right. Up on the ridge when he had first proposed the scheme, everything seemed so simple, straight forward. They needed horses, boots and guns. They were down below.

Suddenly, his priorities had changed.

The man on the floor was coming to. Groaning, but at least he was still alive and would recover. A man facing a charge of buckshot would be cut to pieces. Charlie Bassett's mind was in a quandary. What should he do? Betrayal was hard to acknowledge. His current buddies, or old pals? He was stuck between a rock and hard place.

Sure, he had killed men before. But the cold-blooded murder of a man he had known and called a friend was all wrong. His mind was made up.

Go through with it and their blood would be on his hands. He was now sure that the guy on the floor would meet a similar fate. Could he live with that? Seconds were ticking by. The full attention of both the Mexican and Quintel was concentrated on the cabin door. Any minute it would open, and Will Crawley would step outside.

Crunch time had arrived like the angel of death. No matter what the outcome, he could not allow Quintel to shoot down Will Crawley.

Charlie heard himself voicing his opposition. The words sounded eerie, as if they were being spoken by someone else.

'Why don't we just grab the horses and ride out through the back door, boss? Ain't no need to shoot a man down like this. It don't sit right.'

Quintel spun on his heels. He glared at the speaker. 'And leave two guys eager and willing to chase us down? You crazy? Not only that, we need boots and guns. They ain't about to hand those over willingly.'

'What is thees, Charlie?' protested Fernando in support of the boss. 'It was you who propose plan. Why so against it now?'

'I can't let you kill those guys, Jeb. That must be Will Crawley inside the cabin. This guy's his father, Ike. I only just eyeballed him. We used to be good buddies.'

The decision made, Bassett hefted the jack pole above his head and launched himself at the gang leader.

Jeb Quinel was caught out by the sudden rush. But he was quick to recover. A sharp exclamation of anger gushed from the open mouth as he hauled back on the trigger. The Loomis barked. Fire and death burst forth in an ear-shattering blast of devastation. Bassett was flung back, his hands clawing at the ragged hole in his stomach. The result of both barrels at point blank range was not a pretty sight.

The Mexican finished the job by pinning the twitchy body to the dirt floor with the pitchfork. Charlie Bassett's frame was quivering like a skewered pig. Blood poured from the flapping mouth. Only another vicious jab from the lethal prongs managed to terminate the gruesome spectacle.

Inside their stalls, the horses trembled and whinnied with fear.

'You darned fool,' Quintel cursed at the bent and blooded torso. 'Why in thunderation did you have to be so goddamned loyal?' Smoke twined lazily from the barrels of the Loomis.

He was not bothered about the untimely demise of his lieutenant. It was the fact that the jigger inside the cabin had now been alerted. Getting rid of the critter had suddenly become that much more difficult.

'What in the name of hellfire are we gonna do now?' he railed helplessly.

Dismayed and alarmed by the sudden death of their sidekick, the two outlaws stood staring down at the speared effigy. It presented the macabre appearance of a giant butterfly pinned to a display board.

Moments later a shaky voice called out from the cabin. 'What's going on in there? You alright, Pa?' Fear was evident in Will Crawley's tremulous appeal. 'Is that greaser causing you trouble?'

All were questions that could only be answered if he himself went to investigate. But the young horse tamer was not about to step beyond the portals of the cabin until he knew the score. A gun poked out of the cabin window. Two shots were loosed at the upper section of the barn. More out of apprehensive frustration and ignorance than any hope of resolving the disturbing fate of his father, who was inside.

Quintel rummaged in the elder bronc-peeler's pockets, emitting a yip of satisfaction on extracting a couple of spare cartridges. He pressed them into the empty barrels. In those few minutes he had worked out a plan to give them the edge. It rested on the fact that Will Crawley figured there was only one man involved in the attack he now believed to have been perpetrated against his father.

The gang leader quickly outlined his ploy.

Fernando smiled. He moved across to the window addressing the man inside the cabin. The lyrical cadence floated across the open sward. 'Your *padre* ees a leetle groggy, *señor.*' He held his peace for a few seconds to allow the implications of his announcement to register. 'Come out with your hands high or he is dead buster for sure. I not greedy. A horse and boots is all I need.'

'What was the gunfire all about?' came back the worried reply. 'Is Pa wounded?'

'Just a bump on head, *señor.* Nothing serious . . . for now. We had thee scuffle and gun went off by accident.'

'Bring him out so I can see he's OK,' Crawley ordered after due consideration of the proposal. He did not trust the Mexican, but had little choice in the matter. His pa's welfare had to come first. 'And leave the gun behind.'

'You also come out, *señor*, without weapon,' replied Fernando aiming a wink at his hidden confederate. 'Then you saddle horse for me.'

The two parties emerged from their respective cover simultaneously. Unbeknown to his assailants, during the verbal exchange Ike Crawley had recovered his wits. Yet he still made out the pretence of being dazed and wobbly on his pins. Once outside in the open, he pushed the greaser to one side and hollered to his exposed son. 'Watch out, boy, there's another rat inside with the gun. He's gonna—'

Those were his final words. The deadly blast of the Loomis took him out. The second barrel intended for Will Crawley fell short of its target, merely digging a hole in the sand three feet short of the scrambling peeler, who quickly disappeared back inside the cabin.

Quintel cursed aloud tossing the gun aside as Fernando rejoined him in the barn. He was beginning to wonder if they wouldn't have been better off continuing along the main trail back to Happy Jack. One man down, another dead outside. They were unarmed and still had to get rid of the young horse-tamer. Riding off through the back door on saddled mounts bootless, and without guns or water was not an option to be considered. Will Crawley had to be disposed of. But how?

This time it was Fernando who came up with a plan. And this one had to work.

SEVEN

SMOKESTACK LIGHTNING

Having mulled over the situation, it was now a question of which outlaw was up to the task. In bare feet, only the most resilient would be capable of pulling it off. Fernando's youth and early background in the slums of Nogales meant his feet were harder. He was tough and wiry; the obvious choice.

'You up for this, Fern?' Quintel fixed the Mexican with a firm eye. 'I'm putting all my trust in you being able to pull it off.'

'Fernando Estrela not take on jobs he cannot finish,' was the gritty resolve. 'That *hombre* ees already out of thee picture.'

Quintel nodded. 'It sure was my lucky day saving your hide down in Bisbee.'

'I the lucky one, *patrón*.'

That had been three months before. Estrela had run foul of a Mexican bandit going under the handle of *El Fogonero*. The Fireman had been the cause of a significant blaze that destroyed the house of Estrela's parents over the border in Nogales. Ostensibly, it was in retaliation for an unpaid land grant that had proved to be worthless. Fernando had tracked the bandit to the Arizona town of Bisbee.

The feisty *peon* unwisely challenged the arsonist in his own back yard, namely the Sunrise saloon. The bandit had scoffed at the threat made by this skinny no-account. His men had quickly disarmed the young hornet. He was taken outside and tethered to a wagon wheel. *El Fogonero* sauntered outside ready and eager to deliver a sound thrashing. The long bull whip snapped.

But the twitching serpent never got to spit its deadly venom, being smashed in two by a well-placed bullet. Jeb Quintel and his gang had arrived in town just as the brutal chastisement was about to be conducted. He quickly surrounded the bandit and his men. The leader of the infamous Shadow Riders had a loathing for whip-wielders having suffered a similar fate himself in his youth.

When The Fireman objected in his own language, Quintel wasted no time in fruitlessly requesting a translation. He shot the bandit straight through the heart. The others rapidly saw sense and backed off.

And that was how Fernando Estrela came to join the enigmatic company of owlhooters. And he had since proved to be a resourceful member of the gang. The young Mexican's most recent proposal was clear evidence of that.

All Quintel could do now was watch from the wings, trusting his confederate to carry through the plan of action he had explained. It was now time to play his part. The gang boss hustled over to the window and called to the man inside the cabin. His idea was to distract the buster in order for Fernando to do his bit.

'Looks like we've gotten ourselves a stand-off, fella,' he declared in a self-assured tone intended to display confidence of an outcome to his advantage. The fact that he had no means of repulsing any challenge was thrust aside. 'You in there, and us out here. Neither of us going any place fast. Why don't you just give us what we want and we can call it quits and depart on friendly terms.'

Will Crawley was distraught at the sudden violence and death of his father. He had been unable to hold back the tears. But the killer's carefree attitude and notion that he should surrender effectively cast off the downcast mood. He was filled with hate and anger. Moving across to the shuttered window, he poked the Henry repeater through the tiny shot hole and loosed off a couple of shots.

'That's your answer!' he hollered. 'I've gotten all I need in here. Sometime soon, you bastards are gonna have to come out. Then it'll be me that does the killing.' He backed up the threat with another two shots.

Quintel smiled to himself. The guy was now good and riled, his whole attention focussed on the barn. Another few jibes were tossed out to keep the dupe's mind concentrated. That allowed Estrela to sneak around to the rear of the cabin. There, he gingerly hauled himself on to the pitch-pine roof.

The greatest of care was needed as he inched his way across to the smoking stovepipe. The slightest creak might alert the guy down below.

Quintel followed his partner's every move as the lean young Mexican slowly crept into position. His heart was hammering nervously as he willed the guy onwards.

'Come on, boy,' he murmured to himself. 'You can do it. Just a little bit further.' In the course of urging his confederate onward, Quintel had unwittingly exposed himself through the barn window. A bullet chewed a large hunk of wood from the frame inches from his head. Sharp fragments sliced open his cheek, drawing blood.

He cried out, slapping a hand to the wound. 'Jeez! What the heck!' Quicker than a randy roadrunner, his head disappeared from view.

A raucous chortle from inside the cabin saw the irate gang boss berating himself for his folly. Unable to reply, he prayed that Will Crawley would not cotton to the fact that he had run out of ammunition as he followed Estrela's progress from a more discrete angle. Inch by inch, the Mexican drew closer to his objective. One false move and it could all be over. Half a dozen rifle bullets through the roof would soon dispose of the intended threat.

Finally, he reached the stovepipe.

Removing his shirt, he stuffed it down the metal

tube thus choking off the escaping smoke. It was then a case of crawling to the edge of the roof where it overlooked the front door. With the shutters and doors all closed up, it would not be long before the inmate would be forced out into the open.

The cabin had been purposefully erected with its back against a near vertical rock wall four hundred feet high. With only one entrance and windows that were shuttered, it offered excellent protection against warring tribes of Mescalero Apaches. That protection was about to prove its undoing in the current stand-off.

Inside the cabin, the first Will Crawley knew that he was in danger was the sudden gush of smoke from the cooking fire. It took only seconds for the backdraft to fill the small room with choking and noxious fumes. Coughing and spluttering, he pressed a bandanna to his face.

How had that happened? It did not occur to the young bronc-peeler that skulduggery was taking place above his head. All he knew was that to remain inside the cabin was not an option. He would be overcome within minutes. Clutching the Henry to his chest, he hustled across to the door and dragged it open. A brief pause on the threshold, then he launched his lithe frame out into the open. His intention was to take cover behind the horse trough.

And he would have made it, had not Fernando Estrela been ready for just such a manoeuvre. As Crawley appeared, Estrela launched himself on to his opponent's back. They both went down in a heap. But the Mexican had the advantage of surprise and emerged on top. He did not waste any time. Will Crawley did not know what hit him.

The rusty knife Estrela had secured from the abandoned wagon was driven hard into Crawley's back. Once, twice, three times it rose and fell.

The Mexican stood up. He leaned over the dead man, gasping in lungfuls of air, the knife raised. But there would no further resistance from Will Crawley. The stand-off was over. He threw the gore-smeared blade away as if it was poison, then scrambled back onto the roof and removed the blockage.

Quintel emerged from the barn and walked across to the cabin. Exhibiting a cold disregard for the deceased, he retrieved the knife and wiped it clean on the dead man's shirt, then handed it back to his associate.

Ever the ruthless brigand, Quintel rapidly brushed off the violent confrontation, announcing with a cheery grin that he was hungry. 'There's grub awaiting us inside the cabin, Fern. Seems a pity to waste it. My stomach's rumbling louder than a herd of charging buffalo.'

He laughed. The raucous bellow was rather too loud. It was certainly no expression of amusement, rather a release of taut nerves and strained muscles. Much as he tried to make light of their recent foray, it had taken its toll.

But not enough to affect his appetite.

Not so the Mexican. At that moment, the last thing on Fernando Estrela's mind was filling his stomach. Exactly the opposite, in fact. The undigested beavertail remains were regurgitated in a spasm of lubberly wretching. Another ten minutes passed before he stumbled into the cabin.

Quintel had thrown open the windows to allow the smoke to dissipate.

'Mighty fine stew, Fern,' he commented without noticing his associate's drawn and haggard features. 'Get a plate and fill up. There's plenty left.'

'I theenk stomach need rest and plenty of water first,' he gurgled, hugging the offending portion of his anatomy.

Only then did Quintel heed the man's waxy look.

'You don't look too good, *hombre*,' he muttered pushing the jug of moonshine across the table. 'A hefty slug of this will soon fix you up.'

Fernando complied. He coughed and spluttered as the fiery tipple burned its way down his gullet. But it certainly appeared to do the trick, bringing some much needed colour to his cheeks. He took another swig and immediately felt better.

'What did I tell you?' breezed Quintel. 'Now ladle out some grub and eat up. We have work to do.'

A half hour later and both men were feeling like their old selves.

The first task was to hunt out some suitable footwear in the back room so recently occupied by the Crawleys. It was a strange experience for Estrela to delve through the personal possessions of the dead men. The very thought of the disposal of the three bodies down a convenient ravine was less harrowing now that he had recovered his composure, and he set about carrying out the task.

Quintel was more pragmatic. Guns, ammunition and fresh duds were his priorities, followed by another plate of rabbit stew from the cauldron simmering on the fire.

'Reckon we'll stay here the night, then set off in the morning,' he declared while forking the delicious repast into his mouth with one hand. The other reached for a glass of moonshine. 'By hokey, these guys sure knew a thing or two about living well out here in the wilds. This chow is a sight better than the slop served out at Happy Jack's.'

Fernando nodded in agreement. 'Ees lucky for us you knew about thees place, *patrón*.' His beaming smile dissolved as he thought back. 'Not so good for poor old Mustang, though.'

Quintel lifted his shoulders in a listless apathetic disinterest. 'You shouldn't feel so blue about it. His allegiance ought to have been with the Shadows, not some guys from way back.' To emphasize the point, he punched out the crown of the hat he had taken from Will Crawley. Quintel preferred to wear his headgear Texas fashion. It was a new Stetson. His old one had been shredded by the young horse-tamer following the unwise exposure in the barn. 'A Judas, that's all he turned out to be. The skunk don't deserve any sympathy.'

Once the meal was finished, smokes were lit as each man retreated into his own thoughts. Quintel was already plotting how to avenge his dead brother. That was now his number one priority. Although he also secretly aspired to the status his younger kin had failed to achieve.

EIGHT

WELCOME TO MAVERICK

The last two miles were taken at walking pace. Cole needed time to think, to absorb the terrain. Probing eyes lit upon memorable landmarks. Angel Rock over to his right with its distinctively coned summit; the elongated ridge of sandstone on the left where he had discovered the remains of an abandoned *pueblo* while out hunting; and the towering saguaros everywhere amidst the splay of mesquite, catclaw and tamarisk.

His first sighting of the town itself was the white spire of the church. A lump caught in the back of his throat as, slowly, the rest of the buildings resolved themselves into a familiar amalgam.

Ivor Seagrove's livery stable still occupied the lot beside Swiss Creek. But the town had grown to double its previous size. Buildings of all sizes stretched back from the main street. Some of them looked mighty smart. He drew the sorrel to a halt beneath the overhanging canopy of a cottonwood. Now that he had finally arrived, a nervous tension rippled through his tight frame. He felt like a kid on his first date.

Would Marcia be pleased to see him? A wide, loving smile of welcoming forgiveness lighting up that beautiful countenance. Or would it be a surly frown of disdain? And Joey. Would his son even recognize the sorry excuse of a father who had abandoned him? Now that the time had arrived for facing up to his failings, Cole was reluctant to take the final plunge.

He stepped down and lit up a cheroot. The smoke helped to calm his trembling nerves. At that moment, a wagon trundled across the creek bridge and headed his way. It drew to a halt. The bed of the wagon was filled with farming supplies.

A young guy clad in faded dungarees and a slouch hat called out a cheery greeting. 'Hi there, stranger. Ain't seen you around here before. New to these parts?'

'Guess you could say that,' replied the wary newcomer. He was hedging his bets. No need to disclose any past associations.

'Well you ain't likely to enter a more friendly town in the whole of the territory.' He pointed to a signboard pinned up on another tree. It read *Welcome to Maverick: elevation – 3,226 feet – population 1,257*. This latter had been crossed out and been replaced by 1,259.

The man elaborated. 'A neighbour of mine has just had twins. My wife is expecting our first child in the fall. We sure are looking forward to being a true family.' He held out a hand. Cole took it. The guy's grip was firm and sincere. 'The name's Harvey Cumstick.'

'I'm the Re— Cole Rickard,' the newcomer quickly corrected. He had become so used to being addressed as the Reno Kid that he almost forgot. This chirpy dude had caused his guard to drop, the natural caution to slip. He coughed to hide the lapse in concentration. 'I'm thinking of settling down here myself.'

The hesitancy passed unnoticed. The name clearly meant nothing to Cumstick. The guy must have moved into the valley some time after Cole had left.

'You've made a wise choice, Mr Rickard. Maverick is going places. There's plenty of land for everybody if'n you're into farming or ranching. And there's no animosity between the various factions. We all get along fine. There's even a sheep herder in one of the branch draws to the north. I run a small spread down the valley apiece. The Smiling Face.' He pointed to the brand etched onto his wagon. It matched the guy's beaming grin. 'We're doing pretty well. Got a hundred head of prime Herefords. And I also breed pigs and chickens. Lucy, my wife, grows all our own vegetables in her garden.'

Cumstick was more garrulous than a snake-oil salesman. Cole couldn't resist a smile. But he liked the guy. The rancher was a good advert for the town. Though if truth be told, the listener was a mite jealous. It was more than that. He envied the guy. This young farmer appeared to have the perfect life. Everything that Cole

Rickard aspired to but had so far been unable to hold down.

Once again, the questions loomed.

Would it ever come about? Was he ever going to be permitted to finally bury the Reno Kid? Or was his destiny already predetermined? Forever fated to be a wandering gunfighter, awaiting that inevitable final showdown.

He struggled to maintain a sanguine outlook to keep the gloom from his reply.

'You sure give a good account of the place,' Cole averred, pasting on his best effort at a positive response. 'Let's hope things turn out right for me as well.'

'All you need is an optimistic outlook. It sure has served me well. Nice meeting you, Cole,' replied Cumstick. 'If'n you stick around, we're bound to meet up at the monthly hoedown in the Buckeye saloon.'

Cole's face registered surprise on hearing the name of his old business interest. He covered the slack jawbone with a quick rejoinder. 'This place serve cold beer? My throat's drier than the desert wind.'

'Flush Harry keeps a fine cellar. Best saloon in Maverick. No cardsharps either. Any tinhorns that figure he's an easy touch soon get a burr up their asses.' He chuckled at his indelicacy before slapping the leathers and moving off with a final, 'See you around.'

Cole stubbed out the cheroot and mounted up. So his old partner was still in charge and keeping everyone in line. Cole was still in the dark regarding

Donovan's use of his nickname. He had no inkling that it had been his notoriety that had maintained the peace for so long before that final ignominious confrontation with Wesco Doyle.

His number one priority now was to call in at the Buckeye and seek Harry's help in contacting Marcia and his son. Walking the sorrel down the middle of the main street was an edifying yet disturbing experience. Many things had changed. The town now had street lighting, and all the stores were connected by boardwalks with verandas.

But some things never changed. The name of Chalk Fenton was still emblazoned on the law office signboard. The starpacker was slouching in his chair outside as was his usual custom around midday. Cole pulled his hat low to shade out his features. He had no wish to court attention this early on.

He urged the sorrel quickly past the law office. But the sheriff paid him no heed. Just another itinerant traveller passing through.

Further down was the Buckeye. A much larger sign than previously now graced the two buildings. Donovan had patently acquired the adjoining empty property. Cole wondered if perhaps he had acquired a new partner as well to help fund the enterprise. According to the sign, it now incorporated a dance hall and theatre in addition to the regular saloon.

And it even looked as if a fresh coat of paint had recently been applied. Perhaps Flush Harry had somehow been expecting a visit? Wishful thinking on Cole's part. There was no chance of anybody knowing about his current appearance. He moved across to the hitch rail and dismounted.

Stepping up onto the boardwalk, he paused before entering the saloon and lit up another cheroot. He needed the smoke to settle his nerves, give him chance to figure out a line of approach. After readying himself, he took a step forward and almost collided with a woman hurrying the other way.

'Pardon me, ma'am,' he apologized doffing his hat.

The woman looked up. It was Miss Aveline Beddows. So astounded was she at seeing this disquieting memory from the past, that she dropped the bolts of cloth she was carrying. Cole quickly retrieved the fallen items. The starchy dame had made no secret of her distaste for the infamous bounty hunter when he had begun courting her friend all those years ago. Clearly she was still running up dresses for the local women. And time hadn't softened that austere demeanour. Her beaky snout was still stuck in the clouds. Some things never changed.

But Cole didn't hold a grudge. 'Allow me to help you carry your things. . . .' But he was given no chance to deliver the gallant gesture.

'Wh-what are y-you doing h-here. . . ?' the pedantic spinster blurted out, shocked by this man's abrupt and unexpected appearance. The stammered reaction became more pronounced. 'You're . . . you're . . . It can't be. . . . You should be. . . .'

'How is Marcia?' Cole interrupted without thought for the woman's bewilderment. He assumed it was just a natural surprise at meeting him after five long years.

He was more concerned about other matters than this woman's disbelief at his unannounced return to Maverick. 'Is she in good health? And Joey, how's he?'

He wasn't afforded the opportunity to proffer any more questions. Nor did he receive an answer. The startled woman shook her head, staring at him as if he were some kind of ghost, a macabre denizen impossible to comprehend. She couldn't escape quickly enough. Cole was mystified. The woman appeared to be terrified of him. Scared out of her wits. Surely he hadn't been that much of an ogre.

He launched a puzzled frown at the woman's back. It didn't make any sense.

Shoulders lifted in acceptance. Women were a law unto themselves; it was best for a guy not to even try figuring out their motives. He quickly turned his attention to a more pressing matter.

The front window afforded a panoramic view of the saloon's interior. There he was, standing behind the bar: Flush Harry Donovan, as large as life. He looked much the same, a few extra grey hairs, and that belly was protruding more than it ought. A glass of beer was under close scrutiny. Cole smiled. His old partner always had been a stickler when it came to dispensing the finest quality beverage.

He pushed through the door and gave the room a closer inspection. As expected, the back mirror was highly polished. The gaudy painting of a somewhat scantily clad female now graced the wall above. Otherwise everything appeared the same. It was as if he had only been away a couple of days. He sauntered over to the bar.

'Be with you in a moment,' the saloon owner said without taking his eye off the foaming brew. 'Just checking this delivery is up to standard. The Buckeye takes pride in always serving its customers nothing but the best.'

'Glad to see you're keeping up the high standards,' muttered the newcomer.

The beer checker froze. For a moment he just stood there, stiff as a pikestaff. Then his eyes slowly shifted to regard the speaker. So stunned was he at the vision now before him, that the glass slipped from his hand and smashed on the bar top. The contents spilled across the polished surface, but went un-heeded. Those staring peepers maintained their hypnotic fixation on the newcomer.

Then his mouth began flapping. But nothing emerged.

Cole blinked. His brow furrowed. This was the same reaction as that from Aveline Beddows. Surely he wasn't that much of an unwelcome pariah?

At last, Donovan found his voice. 'Is it really you, Cole? But it can't be.'

Cole was becoming a mite exasperated by this bizarre behaviour. He grabbed Flush Harry's hand and touched it to his stubbly face. 'Feel that, Harry. Whiskers and flesh. It ain't no ghost you're touching.'

'But it can't be. . . . You're supposed to be—'

'What in thunder is going on around here?' Cole's frustration was bubbling over. 'First I have Aveline Beddows figuring I'm some kind of apparition. Now you. What gives, Harry?'

The saloon owner shook off the torpor that had gripped his innards. He called across to a bartender who was clearing some tables. 'Hey, Digweed! Clear up this mess, will you? I got some business to discuss with this gentleman in the back office.'

'Sure thing, boss,' came the drawled reply.

Without another word, Donovan led the way. Once in the privacy of his office, he poured two glasses of whiskey, handed one to his guest and downed the other in a single draught. 'You best do the same, Cole. You're gonna need it.'

'I don't like the sound of this, Harry.' The reply was faltering, hesitant. The drink remained untouched. 'What's been happening here that's so all-fired unsavoury?'

'You ain't gonna like it.'

'Just tell me!' Cole's voice had risen to a barely controlled bark.

'Fact is . . . we all thought you were dead.'

'Dead! How come?'

'And that ain't all.' Donovan swallowed nervously. 'Marcia has remarried. Joey now has a new stepfather that he calls Pa.'

This time it was Cole's turn to display stunned shock. It was total and absolute. He slumped into a chair. The whiskey disappeared down his throat. He held out the glass for a refill. That vanished at an equally fast rate. Only then did Cole Rickard turn back to face his old friend. His face was a blank mask behind which all manner of disparate thoughts were churning.

'You best spill the beans, Harry.'

Donovan sat down behind his desk. He folded his arms thinking how best to explain away such a screwball disclosure.

'The guy's name is Luther Duggan. He arrived in Maverick about a year after you left claiming that the Reno Kid was dead. Everyone was shocked at this announcement. Not least Marcia. Duggan gave the impression of having been in business with you up north in a place called St Elmo, Colorado.'

Cole's body stiffened. His eyes narrowed to thin slivers of blue ice. It had to be his old partner. 'Did this jigger have a broad Irish accent and a lazy squint that gave his face a lob-sided appearance?' he shot back. 'Made him look kind of shifty?'

'That's him,' replied Donovan.

Cole bit down on his lower lip. 'I knew the pesky rat as Lex Dooley. He's even had the gall to keep the same initials.'

'He sure had the gift of the gab,' Donovan continued. 'Still does. Before I knew what was happening he had bought into the saloon. Had all these ideas about expanding the business. Then it was Marcia's turn. He charmed her with all that blarney. She was soon hooked like the rest of us. The guy seemed genuine enough. Had the dough to invest, not to mention a bucket full of charisma that included having young Joey hanging on his every word. Marriage soon followed. After all, as far as everybody here was concerned, the guy was telling the truth. Why should we think otherwise? You were dead, so she was no longer committed.'

'I see you've bought old Jackson's place next door. Was that his idea as well?' The cutting remark was laced with irony.

Donovan shrugged. 'You and me had intended doing that anyway. And it sure was a good move. We run dances and the monthly hoedown. And the top acts from around the country have been booked in.'

This was not what Cole wanted to hear. 'You two seem to have hit it off big time.' The remark emerged as a scathing hit of sarcasm. 'Reckon all that Irish hooey didn't need to talk you around.'

'Now that ain't fair, Cole,' protested Donovan. 'If'n I'd known what the skunk was up to, I'd never have gone along with making him a partner, or letting him go anywhere near Marcia. You know me better than that.'

Cole knew he had overstepped the mark. He apologized, acknowledging that it was his anger that was getting the better of his mouth.

'Sorry about that, Harry. I ain't thinking straight. This varmint has really done the dirty on me. Did he say how I happened to meet this unfortunate end?'

'One gunfight too many.' Donovan's eyes lifted as if to imply it couldn't have been anything else, knowing Cole as he did.

'Guess I asked for that,' came back the sheepish reply.

Donovan smiled to show there were no hard feelings, then continued. 'He reckoned you'd been drinking and got into a fracas with some cowhands. The booze slowed you down when they called you out. Duggan claimed to have tried pacifying the punchers, but their leader wanted to acquire that all-important reputation. Far as we were concerned he had succeeded. The Reno Kid was no more.'

A heavy silence descended over the two old partners. Each was cocooned in his own mind warp.

It was Donovan who broke into the tense atmosphere. The saloon boss was coming to realize how easily he and the rest of the town had been hoodwinked by this charlatan. They had all been taken in by his smooth charm, made to look like naive fools, simple-minded dupes.

He gripped the side of the desk, knuckles blanching with an inner fury.

'It was all a load of flimflam to wheedle his way into our confidence. The guy's a no-good trickster, a fraud. It makes me ashamed of my Irish roots to have believed all that hogwash. I'm beginning to wonder when he intended pulling the plug on me. Vanishing in the night with all our profits.'

Tight features hardened as he concluded the bleak account. 'And to cap it all, he reckoned that your final choking request allegedly urged him to visit Maverick and smooth things over with your wife. Well he's sure done that while ingratiating himself fully into her confidence.'

'Not to mention her bed,' Cole snarled, downing another shot of whiskey.

NINE

SHAKE HANDS WITH THE DEVIL

Cole lurched to his feet and paced the room. The truth bore no resemblance whatsoever to this lurid charade.

It was time to set the record straight.

By the time the Reno Kid arrived in St Elmo, six months had passed following his ignominious flight from Maverick. Surprisingly, he had slotted back into his old profession without much effort. That wasn't to say that he did not regret the fateful actions that had led to that sorry affair.

The question as to whether he would have done anything different was one that had no answer. The die was cast and he had to accept the consequences. For now, at least. Perhaps at some point in the none too distant future he could return and hopefully smooth over troubled waters. But he knew deep down that it would take a long time for the dust to settle.

Reno booked into the Comfort Hotel. Having sampled the bed in his room, he had to agree with the owner's claim that the premises possessed the softest mattresses in Colorado. A solid night's sleep and a hearty breakfast now behind him, he ventured outside. An early mist hung around the tops of the mountains and the air was cool and crisp. St Elmo was high up in the San Isobel Range. Even in summer it was an effort for the sun to drag itself above the rimrock and make its presence felt.

The town was just another gold mining settlement. It had only been in existence for a few years but already it had become the hub of the local area. Supplying mining equipment, the town also acted as the jumping off point for prospectors heading into the surrounding hills.

It had originally been given the prosaic name of Forest City due its being surrounding by dense stands of pine and aspen. The more imaginative appendage stemmed from a council member who had read a popular novel of the day back in 1866 entitled *St Elmo*. It was about the patron saint of sailors. The guy had once been a ship's captain and the name stuck.

In the meantime, another piece of lawless endeavour was beckoning. Reno breathed in the crystal clear ozone then headed across the street for the marshal's office. That was the place where wanted notices were always to be found. Judging by the date on the one he was now studying, it had only just been pinned up. A jasper sporting the flamboyant title of Dirty Dan Pickersgill was wanted for robbery. Reno had never heard the name before.

He scanned the description which indicated that the outlaw had carried out his latest caper only two days before. A regular practice appeared to have served the outlaw well regarding the manner of his skulduggery. Hence, five similar robberies had been ascribed to the same perpetrator.

Removing the notice, Reno knocked on the office door. A muted voice invited him to enter. Marshal Linc Satcher was pouring himself a cup of coffee. He recognized the newcomer immediately.

'Ain't seen you around these parts for a spell, Kid.'

His greeting was even. Not exactly friendly, but neither was it hostile as with many of his contemporaries in other towns. Bounty hunters never quite knew how their search for paid work would be received. A working relationship existed between these two stalwarts that had served both men well in the past.

Their last encounter had resulted in Reno sharing his reward with Satcher due to help given in apprehending Gentleman Jim Swinburn – a shifty gambler and confidence trickster.

'Fancy a cup of my finest Arbuckles?' The marshal didn't wait for a reply. He levered himself out of his chair and wandered across to the ever-bubbling pot on the stove. Pouring a mug of the steaming brew, he passed it across. 'Guess you're here about Dirty Dan.'

The manhunter laid the notice down on the marshal's desk. 'Got any extra information you can give me, Linc?' he asked sipping at the scalding drink. The brew was thick, strong and sweet, just as he liked it.

'Last sighting of the critter was from Lex Dooley. The guy runs the mining equipment store down the street. Pickersgill robbed him in broad daylight three days ago. A couple of bullets chased him out of town, but the critter escaped unhurt. Dooley reckons the cocky braggart stupidly let slip he was heading for Leadville. So like as not he'll go over Woodstock Pass by way of the Sherrod Loop.'

Reno scratched his head. 'I ain't never been that way before. Any help you can give to catch up with this dude would be much appreciated.' The inference was clear. Help given by Linc Satcher would be rewarded. And with the marshal possessing an intimate knowledge of local terrain, his assistance would be vital.

'He's got a three day start,' the lawman averred, handing over a large Havana. 'I reckon your best bet is to take the old Indian trail over the Devil's Horseback.'

The two men lit up, imbibing the aroma and taste of the renowned cigars. Satcher went on to explain the prospective short cut. Both men then went outside and the marshal pointed to a distinctive mountain peak.

'There's a narrow trail up through the trees. But it's clear enough to follow. Always make sure to keep Mount Princeton on your right. By travelling light and replenishing your supplies at Tin Cup and Winfield, you should easily get ahead of him. He'll have to go by Twin Lakes before dropping down into Leadville. That's the ideal spot to nail the bastard.'

'Best if'n I hit the trail perty soon then,' Reno con-cluded. 'Three days is a good start. The only problem is my horse is plum tuckered out. He needs a rest.'

Satcher had the answer. 'Hang on here a minute.'

He went back inside the office and quickly scribbled out a note of authorization.

'Give this to Jake Harlow who runs the Turret livery barn. Tell him that you're doing some work for me.' He offered the bounty hunter a knowing wink. 'Ain't so far from the truth, is it?' As Reno turned away, the starpacker offered a whimsical piece of advice. 'Keep well up wind of Pickersgill. That moniker wasn't granted lightly. The guy has a distinct aversion to soap.'

Reno laughed. 'So it says on the dodger. Do you reckon the knucklehead realized he was leaving his calling card when he pulled all those jobs?'

Satcher shrugged. 'At least it should give you fair warning of his approach.'

Before heading down to the livery, Reno decided to call in at the mining store and find out some more information about the robbery.

Dooley was a bluff rangy Irishman with a brogue to match. A profusion of unruly red hair cascaded from beneath the brown derby perched askew his head. A twitchy right eye gave his face an odd lilt. The other twinkled evocatively and spoke of hidden depths that would only be revealed to his most trusted confidents.

A born salesman, Dooley was eager to draw the new-comer into his confidence. The lyrical cadence was a distinct help in gaining people's trust. He was pleased to meet the renowned bounty hunter. They shook hands. Reno was well versed in the vagaries of human nature, but the Irishman's jovial and affable manner had him hooked.

Dooley explained that he had started out in mining but quickly discovered that serving the needs of others was far more lucrative. 'And to be sure it was a sight less hard on the body.' The hearty guffaw exuded a jaunty humour that did not quite reach his eyes. Reno joined in. He liked the guy. But had he paid more attention to the veiled signs, perhaps history would have followed a different course.

'You catch this varmint, me fine fella, and return the goods,' Dooley promised in a low, conspiratorial manner, 'and you'll find that Lex Dooley will be very grateful.' He did not elaborate, but the hint was that an extra reward on top of the official bounty would be forthcoming.

The manhunter left soon after with a positive impression of the man who was to become his partner . . . and stinger.

Following Marshal Satcher's instructions, Reno managed to reach Twin Lakes in two days. He reckoned that he must now be a good half day ahead of the outlaw. That was always presupposing that Dirty Dan followed an expected route. He had no reason to think otherwise.

Unless, of course, the heist man remembered dropping himself in the mire by mentioning Leadville to the robbed storekeeper. The next few hours would resolve that issue. If'n the guy had deliberately laid a false trail, Reno would be up the creek without a paddle.

All he could do now was lay the trap he had figured out, then wait and hope.

It was around four in the afternoon that the steady drub of hoof beats assailed his acute hearing. Could this be his man?

He peered out from behind a tall aspen to view the open track to the south. The lone rider was wearing a red checked shirt and black leather vest. His wide-brimmed plainsman hid the face, but Reno knew from the description given by the St Elmo lawman, as well as Lex Dooley, that this was his man.

Reno tugged on the rope he had stretched across the trail between two tree trunks. It was tied at chest height, the intention being to unseat a horseman. A watchful rider might just spot the impedance in time. But Pickersgill was likely too sure of himself now to warrant any extra caution. Leadville was over the next ridge, no more than two hours' ride distant. He would be there before nightfall.

Reno hid behind the broad trunk and waited. The pace of the approaching horse never faltered. The danger had not been spotted. Seconds later, a burbled cry of anguish was followed by a dull thud as the upended rider hit the dirt. The ambusher rushed out from cover, six-gun at the ready, but he had no need for any concern. The guy had been knocked out cold.

Quickly, he dragged Dirty Dan into the shelter of the camp he had set up in a small glade some one hundred yards off the main trail. It was a tough task. Pickersgill was a burly dude who clearly didn't believe in skimping his grub. He also exuded a sour aroma redolent of stale booze and sweat. Linc Satcher had not exaggerated; this guy needed the attentions of carbolic and a hot tub.

And Reno would likewise require the deluxe treatment following this caper.

He tied the outlaw securely to a thin trunk, then went in search of the guy's horse. Luckily it had not wandered far, having discovered some succulent grasses beside one of the lakes.

Back in camp Reno searched the saddle-bags for the stolen items but found nothing. Dirty Dan must have stashed them away. Probably, he was amassing a stockpile until such time as he could head for the bright lights of California and live the high life for a spell. Reno would soon find out. A mug of ice-cold water was tossed into the bearded mush of his prisoner.

'What in the name of blue blazes is going on here?' Pickersgill railed as he coughed and spluttered, shaking his head. Only then did the realization dawn that he was fastened up tighter than a calico queen's corsets. 'Who in hell's teeth are you?' he demanded, struggling to get free. It was a fruitless exercise.

'I'm the Reno Kid, the guy that's taking you back to St Elmo to stand trial and earn me a good payoff,' Reno smiled, extracting the Wanted dodger from his pocket. He held it up in front of the scowling captive. The icy grin was instantly replaced by a menacing grimace that augured badly for Pickersgill should his answer be in the negative. 'Now where are all the goods

101

you've stolen?'

'A damned bounty hunter!' rasped the captive. 'Well you can go to hell, mister. It'll be me that sees you facing a jury. I ain't done nothing wrong. You have the wrong man. Now set me free. Then I might decide to forget this ever happened.'

'Wrong answer, Dirty Dan.' Reno smiled when the prisoner's eyes bulged. A pinched nose emitted a lurid sniff of distaste. 'And the name sure fits. Now we can make this easy. Or you and me are gonna fall out big time. Which is it to be?'

'Stuff you, Reno,' snarled the brash outlaw. 'You've got nothing on me. I ain't carrying no stolen goods.'

'That's cos you've hidden the loot. Cough up now and I'll make sure the law hears about your co-operation.'

But still Dirty Dan maintained a stoical disdain and refused to co-operate. 'I've heard all about you, Reno. But it don't scare me none.'

'So what have you heard?'

'That you're a no-good yeller backshooter.'

The sneering insult saw the Kid grabbing a hold of the outlaw's shirt. His revolver snapped to half cock and jammed into Pickersgill's neck. His verbal response was a barely controlled hiss. 'And you'll also have heard that guys like me have the choice of how we deliver up scum like you. Now figure out which it's gonna be for you if'n that loot don't come my way.' The gun went to full cock, its hard barrel matching the cold, merciless gaze.

The outlaw was staring death in the face.

'OK, OK!' he croaked, his heart racing at fifty to the dozen. The brigand perceived that there was no mercy in the flinty regard. Refuse to co-operate now and he would assuredly be strumming with the Devil. 'OK, OK, y-you win,' he stuttered. 'I'll take you to where I've buried the loot.'

The hideaway proved to be a cave up a side gulch that had once been home to a grizzly bear. And there was a considerable amount of gold, paper money and various pink-tied documents stashed away. It was one of these latter that was to draw the Reno Kid into the underhanded machinations of Lex Dooley.

Pickersgill revealed that he had been planning one last job in Leadville before heading for California. So Reno's assessment of the guy's plans had been correct.

No problems were encountered on the ride back to St Elmo. At the first night's camp Reno cleaned himself up in a creek. Dirty Dan was kept securely trussed up then forced to endure the same treatment under the watchful eye of his captor.

Once his prisoner had been delivered to the marshal's office, Reno called in at the bank to collect his reward, a portion of which found its way into the marshal's pocket. Both of them then moseyed across to the saloon to celebrate their windfall.

Reno later went to visit Lex Dooley, who was over-joyed to retrieve his stolen goods. The storekeeper was as voluble as before. And he kept to his word. One of the documents was the filing claim to a gold mine he had won in a poker game. And it was this that found the Reno Kid enmeshed within the spider's web.

'I've had it assessed and transferred into my name,' Dooley enthused, prodding the affidavit. 'And I'm giving you the chance to invest in what is already a lucrative prospect. With your input, we'll be able to buy the heavy drilling equipment to really make this mine pay big bucks.' He looked at the somewhat bewildered potential new partner. 'It's a sure-fire winner. But it needs added capital that I don't have. So what do you say?'

Reno's furrowed brow indicated he was tossing over the pros and cons of the proposed joint venture. His head was rather thick after one too many at the saloon. Perhaps if he had been more alert, Dooley's persuasive eloquence would have been subject to greater scrutiny. He merely skimmed over it. A few peremptory nods of understanding and he was more than happy to give his consent.

'Sounds good to me, Lex,' Reno declared rather diffidently. There was only one thing that was bothering him. 'Only problem is, I don't know a thing about mining.'

The Irishman hawked out a jaunty guffaw. 'You don't need to. We hire in the labour to do all the hard work. All we have to do is sit back and rake in the profits.'

The Kid thought for a moment trying to gather his thoughts. It would make life a lot easier. And this guy seemed genuine enough.

Everything would be above board and legal. How could he lose?

Prophetic last words that were to cost him dear.

Nevertheless, he signed on the dotted line confirming the deal.

TEN

SNAKE BITE

Everything went smoothly for the first six months of their association. Reno had taken to overseeing work carried on at the mine. Ore samples had indeed proven their worth. And the seam was highly productive. The money in the bank was mounting up and all seemed well with the world.

With Reno away from civilization for substantial periods of time, the opportunities for young guns to challenge his reputation were scant. He had reverted to calling himself Cole Rickard. Another six months and there would be enough dough stashed away in the company safe to enable him to sell his share of the mine. That would let him move away and start up afresh where nobody would recognize the name of the Reno Kid.

Maybe he would head back East to Chicago, or New

106

York. Perhaps even a trip over to Europe would be forthcoming. The options were unlimited for a man of visible means. He still thought about his wife and son, though less and less as time passed. Dreams filled his head. But like all bubbles, they were bound to burst eventually.

It happened one Sunday morning.

Dooley wanted him to make a personal inspection of the mine. A new territorial ruling had been issued that stated all mines operating above a certain threshold had to receive an annual inspection to determine safety procedures. Apparently, too many unwarranted accidents had been reported and the authorities needed to act. A wire had been received from the Colorado Mining Legislature stating that a surprise visit was planned for the coming week.

Urgent attention was, therefore, necessary to ensure their operation complied with the rules.

'Just make certain there are no loose props, or rotten beams. Anything you find, let me know and I'll arrange for them to be replaced before the inspectors arrive.'

The urgency in Dooley's voice and his stoic regard were at odds to the normally light-hearted banter. The serious tone was a convincing enough argument for Cole. His partner's final declaration was the catalyst that spurred him to abandon his day off. 'Should those inspectors find anything, we could be closed down for months. All our profits will be used up complying with their durned regulations. I'm counting on you to make sure that don't happen.'

During that last six months the mine had been operating at full capacity thanks to the new equipment. And Cole had become well versed in the industry and its operation. So he felt well able to spot any safety hazards that might be present.

Dooley's choice of days had been deliberate. The workers always headed into town on Saturday night and slept off their carousal during the day of rest on Sunday. As a result, the mine would be devoid of any potential witnesses to what he had in mind for his gullible partner.

Cole set off first thing on Sunday morning. The mine was a two hour ride up into the hills behind St Elmo. There was a steady climb through the stands of pine before he branched left along Staghorn Gulch. At the top end was the Exchequer Mine. Cole had no reason to figure there was any skulduggery afoot. His partner was a more than credible charlatan. All that was on his mind was checking the mine out for any abnormalities.

Had he been thus disposed, perhaps he would have spotted Dooley dogging his trail. But Cole had grown lax in such matters. He had no reason to suspect that anything untoward was afoot. And the trickster made certain to stay well back to prevent such an occurrence. He knew exactly where his unsuspecting partner was headed.

Cole tethered his mount outside the wooden shack that served as an office and cantina. Taking a tallow brand he hurried across to the entrance, first checking the stanchions for firmness and wear. A match was applied to the torch after which he moved into the main body of the diggings. He followed the narrow-gauge horse-drawn railroad, carefully checking every post, roof support and anchoring cable.

They had even installed a steam pump to extract the water that dribbled through cracks in the rock to prevent flooding at the lower levels.

His estimate was that a thorough search should occupy no more than a couple of hours. There were plenty of spare torches scattered throughout the galleries so spotting any unsafe sections should pose no problems. A pot of paint and a brush were held in the other hand to mark those areas needing attention.

Dooley arrived fifteen minutes later. A crafty smirk broke the stern look as he spotted the tethered sorrel. A quick look around informed him that his associate was inside the mine.

'This is where you and me part company, sucker,' he muttered to himself. 'Permanently. Then I can go pick up where you left off.'

One night in a moment of drunken petulance, Cole had disclosed his innermost regrets concerning his past life in Maverick. The whole sorry episode had come pouring out. The perfect wife and son, a half share in a saloon with a trustworthy partner, a respected position in a town that was going places. In short, the ideal life, the epitome of everything a man of his dubious reputation could desire.

And it had all been destroyed by an arrogant need to prove his machismo. Tears had welled up in his eyes.

But the next day, there was no recollection of the piteous outpouring of grief. Nursing a sore head he mumbled, 'Did I make a fool of myself last night, Lex? Always was too darned talkative after a few drinks.'

'Like what?' asked Dooley nonchalantly.

'Oh! You know, things about my past?'

'To be sure, nothing at all, pard,' replied the breezy Irishman. 'It was mostly about all those young turks who have tried to outgun you.'

Cole sighed. 'Some'n a guy struggles to live down. Be glad you ain't so burdened, Lex. It's a damn blasted yoke around my neck, to be sure.' He chuckled at the inept effort to copy his partner's lyrical brogue.

Lex Dooley chuckled along with him. But his eyes remained flat and cold as a dead fish. He had remembered every last word. And now he intended to capitalize on that private exposé. Dooley had always hankered after such a life himself. Now he had the chance. By relating a plausible sob story, he was confident of being able to ingratiate himself into Maverick society.

The key to carrying out the dastardly ploy was dynamite. Dooley had read up on its safe use and obtained practical advice from miners purchasing the explosives from the store. He carried the sticks over to the mine entrance and proceeded to secure them to the appropriate beams and cracks in the rock.

Peering inside the dark recess, he listened intently for any sound that would betray his partner's presence. Apart from the constant drip, drip from overhead, silence pervaded. Reno was well inside.

A mirthless smirk cracked the macabre Irish facade. 'This is going to be one showdown from which there

110

will be no escape for the Reno Kid,' he muttered under his breath.

Sufficient fuse wire was attached to the sticks of dynamite, which he fed back across the open ground to a safe haven behind a tailings heap. A match was applied to the fuse. Then he settled back and watched it fizzle and spit, chewing away like a hungry rat scuttling across the sandy shelf towards the final denouement.

'So long, Kid.'

Moments later a series of cataclysmic explosions ripped apart the entrance to the Exchequer Mine. Rumbling and growling like an angry giant, the mountain shuddered in protest. There was no denying the brutal efficiency of high explosives. Broken rock tumbled down, completely blocking the mouth. A huge dust cloud bubbled and fermented out of the shattered entrance to the once vibrant mine.

Dooley was mesmerized, stunned at the wholesale destruction he had wrought. But it was only a temporary aberration. He punched the air and cheered at the total success of his heinous endeavour. Nobody could survive that. Not even the legendary Reno Kid. He spat on the ground.

'You were just too trusting, Kid,' he sighed, almost feeling sorry for the poor sap. 'But a man has to take his chance where he can in this tough life. Winner takes all.'

There was no remorse in the callous indifference to his partner's fate. It was merely a question of the survival of the most devious. And Lex Dooley had hit he jackpot in that respect. He wasted no more time in contemplating his future. That would come on the long ride south to Arizona. First he needed to empty the safe and make a swift departure before the alarm was raised the following day.

But Dooley had made a fatal error of judgement when luring the Reno Kid into his sticky tentacles. By giving the entire running of the mining enterprise over to his new partner, the Irishman had shown little interest in its daily operation. No questions were asked just so long as the profits kept rolling in.

As a result he knew nothing about the safety procedures that Reno had installed on the advice of his new foreman. Hardrock Harris had suggested that a couple of narrow air ducts be driven down from the hillside above the mine to provide fresh air and a means of escape, primarily for noxious gases. But also for men as a last resort should there be a cave-in.

That oversight on Dooley's part was to be his Achilles heel.

The first Cole knew that something was wrong was the rumble of shifting rock. It was preceded by a muted roar that sounded suspiciously like an explosion. He had heard enough of those over the last six months. But how could that be happening? Being a Sunday morning, the mine site was empty.

The groaning and shaking rapidly grew more pronounced. Could it be an earthquake? Dust funnelled down the shaft in which he was working. His blood froze. A mining collapse was not something he had experienced before. It felt and sounded terrifying.

112

All around him the wooden beams were cracking under the strain. Rocks came tumbling down from the fractured roof.

Panic threatened to overwhelm him, freezing his muscles. But the human survival instinct kicked in and found him scrambling towards an upturned ore wagon. Death stared Cole Rickard in the face. He was convinced it had arrived in force when he blacked out.

Sitting in the back office of the Buckeye saloon, Cole paused to light up a cheroot. During the lucidly eloquent description of his adventures since leaving Maverick, Flush Harry Donovan had listened intently. The bottle of whiskey was almost empty. With the grim revelation reaching the point where his old friend was about to enter the welcoming arms of the Reaper, he felt compelled to interject.

'How in thunder did you manage to get out of that scrape? Even the irrepressible Reno Kid must have assumed that his end had arrived.'

'You sure ain't wrong there, buddy,' Cole declared emptying the rest of the whiskey into a glass and imbibing a liberal slug. 'Those rocks were coming down every which way. I had no chance of avoiding them. I ended up with a dislocated shoulder.' He gingerly flexed the injured appendage. 'It still gives me jip in cold weather.'

Then he removed his hat. Donovan couldn't restrain a startled grunt. A livid purple scar was etched into his friend's head above the left ear where hair now refused to grow. Cole ran a finger across the dent in his skull.

'How I survived that is anybody's guess. The Good Lord must have been on my side that day.'

'So how did you get out of that hell hole?'

Stunned by the sudden thump on the head, Reno managed to crawl under the wagon before he passed out. Some time later he came round with a stinking headache. But at least he was still alive. It could have been minutes, hours, or even days. The blackness was complete. All the torches had been extinguished. The only thing that the victim recalled was that he was close to one of the air shafts.

And that was how he managed to escape from the jaws of certain death. He was only able to use one hand due to the dislocation but metal rungs had been inserted for just such an eventuality. With no light, the assent of the narrow flue was literally a matter of touch and go. It was still daylight when he reached the plateau above. The bone-jarring ordeal had taken the better part of two hours.

He pulled his bruised and battered frame out onto the hard rock surface. And there he lay, gulping down lungfuls of oxygen that tasted like pure nectar. Feeling faint and light-headed, the pain in his shoulder throbbed abominably. Rheumy eyes slowly opened, trying to absorb the near-death experience.

According to the sun's position in the azure sky it was around three in the afternoon. He had faced down gunslingers and not batted an eyelid. But almost getting buried alive under a collapsing mine was enough to frighten the Devil himself. His stomach wretched at the thought.

There came a time when he knew that remaining on the exposed plateau was not an option. Scavenging buzzards were circling overhead. He had to reach civilization, or death would surely claim him. After the mind-boggling ascent of the airshaft, there was no way he intended that happening without a fight.

A descent back to ground level was impossible. The acclivitous face of the rock wall precluded any such attempt. The only alternative was to head north and hope to join the main Leadville-Salida trail.

He found a rock pool to slake his thirst and clean up his wounds, of which there were numerous. Then he set off. The trail was fifteen miles as the crow flies. It ought to take no more than a couple of days in this terrain.

In effect, it took him five days of gruelling toil, living off berries and the odd rabbit shot with his revolver. He finally stumbled out onto the trail just as a team of freight wagons was passing. Exhaustion had claimed his tormented body. He finally came round some three days later in the hospital at Salida.

The dislocated shoulder had been re-set but ached abominably. And the head wound had needed a dozen stitches. Apart from that he had come through the ordeal surprisingly well. The doctor in charge released him after two weeks under the proviso that a period of convalescence was needed for another two weeks. Following three days of inactivity, Reno was edging for a return to St Elmo.

The question uppermost in his mind concerned the cause of the mine collapse.

ELEVEN

DEFANGED

The shock hit Reno like an express train on learning that his partner had scarpered and taken all their savings. The safe lay wide open. It was completely empty. Nobody knew where Dooley had gone. Reno's sudden re-appearance in the mining town merely compounded the puzzling enigma. The unpaid mine workers were disgruntled, but nobody else in St Elmo had been affected. Sympathy was expressed but little else.

He reported the gruesome incident to the town marshal, but there was little that could be done with the perpetrator having disappeared.

A trip up to the mine enabled him to piece together the macabre course of events. Remnants of the dynamiting told their own story. Reno cursed his folly at being duped by the silver-tongue blackguard. How could he have been so easy to fool, so gullible?

It was the Irish blarney. The guy sure knew how to spin a tale.

And he had exercised the same slick glibness upon the citizens of Maverick.

But it was worse than that. Dooley had been prepared to kill his partner in a most hideous manner to attain his loathsome goal.

The recollection made Cole see red. He hammered a bunched fist on Flush Harry's desk. Donovan's green parrot, a reminder of his Irish heritage, squawked loudly in protest at being roused. That was one of the reasons the saloon owner had accepted the charlatan Dooley's explanation without too much effort; the shared culture had a lot to answer for.

Cole ignored the tetchy bird as another slug of whiskey slid effortlessly down his gullet. It helped to calm his wrangled nerves.

So what to do now?

'Duggan is due here' – Harry looked at his watch, checking it with the ticking timepiece on the wall – 'in thirty minutes. We have a meeting to discuss changing our supplier of beer.'

Cole smiled. 'Well it's sure gonna be a meeting he never expected.'

'How do you figure on playing this, Cole?' Donovan's voice was edged with an uncertain waver. He took it for granted this guy was itching for a showdown where gunplay was likely to be involved. That was the last thing Flush Harry wanted. 'I sure don't cotton to a shootout in the Buckeye.'

Cole's reply was unexpected and initiated a sigh of relief.

'Neither do I, Harry. Much as I'd like to fill the critter with a gut full of lead, those days are over. I intend doing everything according to the letter of the law.' His insistence that the infamous Reno Kid's past was buried seemed heartfelt and genuine. 'Sure, I'll confront him. Then I'll march the bastard over to the sheriff's office. Let Fenton sort it out. Attempted murder ought to merit a long stretch in the pen. Not to mention bigamy. Last I heard this territory had no plans to go the way of Utah with those wife-collecting Mormons.'

Over the next few minutes they quickly thrashed out a ploy to catch Lex Dooley, or Luther Duggan as he now called himself, on the wrong foot.

The parrot seemed to agree with their plan. 'That's the way to do it! That's the way to do it!' came the effusive chuckle as the two men returned to the barroom.

It was agreed that Cole should conceal himself behind a velvet drape on the upper veranda. Donovan, meanwhile, would greet his new partner from behind the bar. The saloon man was adamant that the use of a gun would be from him alone, and only to get the drop on the blackguard. Shooting would be a last resort should he resist.

The hollow sound of the wall clock chiming the half hour brought the participants of the confrontation to a height of acute tension. All eyes focused on the Buckeye's front door. The regular patrons were kept in the dark about the coming showdown. It would only have heightened tensions and given the game away.

A long minute passed before a measured tread heralded the arrival of the trickster. Cole peered from
behind the heavy drape. He was surprised on suddenly
being confronted by the snake. Dooley was wearing a
smart tailor-made suit with white linen shirt and black
necktie secured by a diamond stickpin. And all pur-
chased with stolen money. Cole was seething.

He now regretted having left his guns in Flush
Harry's office.

Then again, perhaps that was a wise decision.

Dooley strolled across to the bar acting as if he
owned the place. The cocky strut was no idle performance. He had taken over from Cole Rickard,
assuming his role in every respect. The skunk had
every reason to sport the beaming smile of greeting.

Bestirring himself, Cole struggled to control his
temper as he emerged from cover. Slowly he began to
descend the stairs. Dooley was facing away from his
cheated one-time partner.

'You seem to be doing mighty well for a no-good
thief and fraudster, Lex.' The remark was delivered in
a flat monotone making its impact all the more effective. The general babble of conversation was stilled as
all eyes turned towards the speaker as he descended
the stairs. 'I'm kinda wondering how you came by that
good fortune. Care to enlighten these good folks?'

Dooley froze. There was no mistaking that evenly
measured voice. In the flick of a sidewinder's tongue
the question flashed across his brain as to how the
Reno Kid had managed to extricate himself from that

death-dealing explosion. But it was only momentary.

Any normal dude would have been transfixed by the sudden challenge. But not Lex Dooley. The cat was well and truly out of the bag. His odious trickery had been uncovered. There was only one option left. And he took it.

Unaware that momentous events were unfolding around her, Polkadot Sal, one the show girls, had wandered into the bar. Rehearsals for a forthcoming performance had just finished in the theatre next door.

'Pull me a jar of beer, Digweed,' she said in a croaky voice. 'My throat is dry as dust after all that warbling.'

The girl was not given the opportunity to assuage her thirst. Dooley saw his chance and took it. He hauled out a Colt Lighting hidden in a purpose-made shoulder holster and pumped a couple of shots at the unarmed man on the stairs.

Luckily for Cole his accuracy was awry. The bullets chewed slivers of wood from the banister rail inches from where Cole was standing. He dropped to the floor.

Without waiting for a reaction to his gunplay, Dooley grabbed the singer and jabbed the barrel of the pistol into her swanlike neck. He then backed away towards the door. 'Any of you critters follow, and the dame is dead meat.' Another bullet encouraged the saloon occupants to stay well back.

'The rat means it,' Cole shouted. 'He's capable of anything.'

Outside on the street, there was only one other

121

horse beside his own. Dooley recognized it as the sorrel owned by Reno. He slugged the girl over the head and tossed her to one side like a discarded rag doll. After mounting his own cayuse, he hauled off with the gun through the saloon window until it clicked on empty.

Then, leading the sorrel behind, he dug in the spurs and galloped out of town, only abandoning the animal when he was well clear.

All hell had broken loose in the Buckeye. Men emerged from cover. All attempts to calm things down were ignored as they struggled to come to terms with the sudden violence that had erupted in their quiet town. Only the raised voice of Flush Harry announcing that drinks were on the house brought the panicking throng to order.

Cole pushed his way through the dense mass of humanity surging over to the bar. On the street, he helped the injured girl to her feet and sat her down on a chair. Harry soon joined him. He called for the swamper to go fetch the doctor.

'Boy, I never reckoned on him acting that way,' he stuttered out, still bemused by the sudden turnaround of their plan.

'He sure had me fooled as well,' agreed Cole, who had been equally startled by the braggart's quick-witted reactions.

'Did you see which way he went, Sal?' Donovan asked the still woozy songstress. She groaned but managed to point a wavering hand in the direction of the setting sun.

'The guy even had the quick-wittedness to take my

horse so I couldn't follow,' Cole railed angrily, having being caught out once again.

'Take my horse,' Donovan offered. 'He's well rested in the corral out back. And you bring that skunk back. I don't care how you do it. The rat's gonna pay dear for making idiots of us all.'

Cole wasted no further words on fruitlessly berating himself. He thanked his friend and hustled round to the rear of the Buckeye to find a large bay mare munching on a nosebag. The horse needed saddling, which wasted more time. Swinging the animal around he pounded off in the direction indicated by Polkadot Sal.

Unlike Dooley, Cole was well acquainted with the local terrain. He quickly figured out that the fleeing Judas would stick to the main Tucson highway. There was a little-used back trail that led over Turkey Flats that would bring him out ahead of the charlatan. He was pretty certain that Dooley would not be aware of it. Half a mile west of Maverick, he branched off down a shallow arroyo.

Pushing the strong bay to its limits, he kept up a punishing pace. All he could do now was hope that his supposition was correct. After an hour of hard riding, Cole rejoined the main trail. The only trouble was he was unarmed. In the heat of the moment the legendary gunfighter had forgotten to pack his hardware.

A desperate search along the edge of the rutted highway soon provided the luck he sought. A rocky ledge above the roadway offered the perfect spot for an ambush. He concealed the bay behind some boulders then scrambled up on to the lofty perch. It afforded a fine view back along the trail.

But Lady Luck has a habit of removing her favours. A sandstorm was brewing from the east. Swirling dust devils danced and cavorted, becoming ever more frenetic in their antics as the storm gathered strength. If it continued directly toward Cole's position, he would be overwhelmed and Lex Dooley could easily escape in the enveloping blizzard.

The fleeing Irishman must also have sensed that he might be caught out and forced to hunker down. He spurred the horse onward, trying to outrun the storm. It was a bold yet reckless manoeuvre. Unseen obstacles could easily cause a fall.

Cole's narrowed gaze struggled to pierce the increasingly opaque gloom. The growing howl of the wind-ravaged sandstorm made it near impossible to see anything else. An approaching rider's hoof beats would be muffled and incoherent.

Cole only became aware of his adversary's close proximity when he saw Dooley's horse tear a hole in the ochre wall. He was no more than fifty yards away and due to pass directly beneath Cole's crouched situation.

The storm now came to his rescue. Dooley had taken heed of the high possibility that he might take a tumble and slowed accordingly to a steady trot.

Cole prepared himself for the leap of a lifetime. His whole body tensed. Judging the moment right was essential. As the rider passed by, he dropped onto the cantle behind him, at the same time swinging a punch at his head. Both men were thrown to the ground in a heap of tangled arms and legs. Having the advantage of surprise, Cole was first on his feet. He dragged Dooley up and delivered a couple of short jabs to his jaw.

The guy staggered back, but he soon recovered. Shaking off the sudden attack, he threw himself at his attacker and bore him down. Both men rolled about in the swirling maelstrom hammering at each other's bodies. Fists flew before Dooley managed to scramble out of reach. He drew his pistol and aimed point blank at his advancing opponent. Once again Cole Rickard stared death in the face.

And once again he was able to thwart the Reaper's invitation.

Dooley had forgotten to reload his revolver. He threw the useless hunk of metal at Cole's head but it was easily evaded. This time it was Cole's turn to gain the upper hand. He sunk a right fist into Dooley's midriff finishing with an uppercut that snapped the critter's head back. A final solid drive and the scheming toad was laid out cold.

Cole sank to the ground. But this was no time to linger. The sandstorm was increasing in force. He quickly tethered the unconscious man with his own lariat and dragged him under a rocky overhang. There they hunkered down to await the storm's passing. Sandstorms can last for days, or blow themselves out in a matter of minutes. This one lasted about half an hour before veering away to the south.

They had been lucky. The sun once again made its presence felt.

Securing Dooley to his saddle, Cole led him back along the main highway on the return trip to Maverick.

Lex Dooley had little to say for himself. He had been caught out bang to rights. No excuses were offered; no regrets expressed. But worst of all, he felt no remorse for the heinous actions he had perpetrated, the lives he had tainted with his abject chicanery. Cole felt only contempt for the guy.

He delivered him to the sheriff, who was more than a mite surprised to witness his prisoner walking into the jailhouse.

'Guess I've lost that bet I had with Harry,' he muttered in a rather glum voice that was accompanied by a cheery smile as he locked Dooley in a cell. Cole gave the remark a quizzical frown. 'Reckon I had you all wrong, Cole. Once a gunslinger always … as they say.' He held out a hand. Cole gladly accepted it. 'I was wrong and Harry was right. My betting was that you'd bring this jasper back strapped over his horse. You sure appear to have changed your ways.'

TWELVE

BAD NEWS
TRAVELS FAST

Harry Donovan insisted that his old buddy should have the best room on the top floor of the saloon. Once he had settled in, the two friends went downstairs and sat at one of the tables.

'Much obliged, Harry,' Cole said. 'I hadn't figured on the guy being such a slippery fish. He almost caught me out again.'

'It's the least I can do for an old friend,' Harry enthused, pushing a full bottle of five star brandy across the table. 'You've brought back that conniving weasel without a shot being fired. I don't know how you managed it, but the town is grateful. If'n there's anything else you need, just say the word.'

Cole's manner was subdued. He did not feel the same elation as that exuded by Flush Harry. The saloon owner quickly picked up on the tight atmosphere. He frowned. 'Some'n else bothering you, Cole?'

'I need to see Marcia,' he murmured. 'Do you think you could arrange a meeting? It will allow me to explain. Persuade her that I'm a changed man. Then, if'n she still can't see a future for us, I'll leave town straight away.'

Donovan protested. 'There's no need for that, Cole. Now that Dooley is out of the frame, we could join up as partners again. Why not stick around and see how things go? She's a headstrong woman. And you never know. She might change her mind.'

'If'n she don't,' sighed the downcast man, 'I couldn't stay knowing Marcia was so near yet so far.' Then he bucked up some. 'But that's only if'n she rejects me again. As you say, she might have softened towards me. So how about that meeting?'

'Leave it to me,' Donovan promised getting to his feet. 'I'll go see her right now.'

While he was awaiting the all-important liaison, Cole's nerves twanged and jerked. He was on tenterhooks, unable to settle.

The saloon door opened. His eyes immediately swung expectantly towards the sound of creaking hinges. But it was only a young boy of around eight years of age. He rushed in brandishing a wooden pistol. Hunched down, he adopted the stance of a gun-fighter on the prod. Peering around he hustled over to the nearest table, which so happened to be that occupied by Cole.

'Stick 'em up, mister,' the boy ordered. 'I've got you

covered. Move a muscle and I'll drill you.' His stern look brought a smile to Cole's face, which he attempted to wipe off by obeying the brisk command.

'Don't shoot, partner,' he blubbed effecting the cowed recoil of a beaten villain. 'You've sure gotten the drop on me. I'll come quietly.'

'OK, let's go.' The toy gun wagged. 'I'm taking you over to the sheriff and claiming the reward. I'm a bounty hunter.' He squared his narrow shoulders, preening as if it was the most noble of professions.

'What's your name, mister?' Cole asked. 'Guess I need to know who it is that's arrested me.'

'I'm Joey and—'

But that was as far as it went. At that moment, a woman entered the saloon. Cole sucked in his breath. It was Marcia.

She called across to the boy. 'How many times have I told you not to come in here?' she admonished the youngster. 'This is no place for a boy to be playing. Now come outside this minute.' Her strict tone left Joey in no doubt as to who was calling the shots now.

'Oh, Ma,' he grumbled. 'I wasn't doing no harm. Ain't that right, mister?' He turned, appealing for this man's support.

Cole's gaze met that of his wife. Marcia flinched on recognizing the familiar profile of the man she had long since thought was dead. But her face remained impassive, giving nothing away.

'Do as your mother says, Joey,' he counselled in a measured way. 'She's right. You shouldn't be playing in a saloon.'

Head hanging on his chest, the boy turned to shuffle away. Cole ruffled his hair. 'And don't worry. I'll make sure to give myself up to the sheriff and tell him it was you that made me see the error of my ways.'

That brought a smile to the boy's face. Perking up, he strutted out the door to resume his hunt for outlaws and brigands elsewhere.

Marcia cautiously approached the table. 'And have you seen the error of your ways, Cole?' she posited, sitting opposite this man who had once meant so much to her. 'Or, like Joey, is it just a charade?'

'I came back specially to try and sort things out between us,' Cole averred, reaching across to hold her hand. She did not remove it. 'He seems like a fine boy. You've brought him up good. I never for one minute reckoned on my ex-partner taking over my life. It came as just as much a shock to me as everybody else around here.'

'Harry told me all about it on the way over here.' She went on to explain how Dooley had ingratiated himself into her affections. 'I would never have succumbed to his odious charms if I'd known for one minute that you were still alive. But you never contacted me. So what was I to think?'

'I don't blame you,' Cole replied. 'But once I'd left Maverick under that cloud, the only way to handle it was go back to my old ways. Then I met Lex Dooley. He had been robbed by one of the wanted villains I delivered up to the law. Going into partnership with him helped me shuck the bounty hunter reputation.'

His head drooped. 'Although it never really goes

away.' He was thinking about his most recent encounter and the unforeseen demise of Frank Quintel. 'I can only hope that with your help, I can settle down again. And this time I'll make every effort to be a proper husband and father. That is if'n you can see it in your heart to forgive me. Harry wants me to resume our partnership in the Buckeye. No guns. Just an accounts book and pen. Those will be the tools of my trade from here on if you'll have me back.'

Marcia needed time to think about what he had said. He certainly appeared genuinely contrite. 'That's good news, Cole. I heard how you brought in Luther and I believe what you say. If I agree to make a fresh start, don't let me down again.'

Cole did not enlighten her that he would have used his guns to their full effect had he been so armed. Such a confession was best left unspoken, as were the other unsavoury elements blighting the last five years. He had no wish to rebuild bridges that had not been broken.

The relaxing sound of his wife's voice was a mellifluous lullaby to his ears. The ardent look spoke of a love rekindled. Her touch, the squeezing of a hand, caused his heart to beat faster. Could it really be true that all was forgiven? It appeared so. His whole being buzzed with elation. This called for a celebration.

But it was not to be.

Just when it appeared that he had his future mapped out, the Devil once again stepped in to stir up the dregs of his past.

A cowboy burst through the doors of the saloon.

The guy looked as if he'd been riding at a hell-for-leather pace. His clothes were caked in trail dust, which he attempted to brush off with his hat.

'Looks like you have a hornet up your ass, Buzz,' remarked one onlooker.

Buzz Fetterman had just delivered a couple of prized bulls to Hawk Tamblin who operated the Tumbling T ranch near Safford. He had ridden hard back to Maverick to deliver some extremely disquieting news.

'Give the guy a drink,' suggested someone else. 'Looks like he could use one.'

'Make it a cold beer,' said Fetterman stumbling over to the bar. 'You ain't gonna like what I have to say.'

Digweed quickly pulled the drink, which was downed in a single draught. 'So what's this bad news that's so all-fired important?' demanded the bartender.

The whole saloon had swung to face the newcomer. Mordant curiosity and outright fear were stamped across staring faces. Everybody was on tenterhooks when it was revealed that what he had to impart was allegedly bad for them all.

'After delivering the bulls to the Tumbling T, I called in at the Wayfarer saloon in Safford,' Fetterman began taking a pull at his refilled jug. 'Only intended to stay for a couple, but I met up with some old pals I hadn't seen for a spell. We got to jawing. You know how it is.'

'Just get to the point, Buzz,' interjected Digweed. 'We ain't interested in an account of your idle chin-wagging.'

Fetterman huffed some. 'Only setting the scene for

what I have to say,' countered the irked cowpoke.

Then he launched into the meat of what he had witnessed.

THIRTEEN

JEB QUINTEL'S PROMISE

The cowpuncher was standing at the bar in the Wayfarer saloon when two drifters walked in. His pals from the Tumbling T had left and Buzz was finishing off his beer and minding his own business. The sale of the bulls had gone as planned. The few drinks had been well earned. Perhaps he would stay over in a hotel. The boss couldn't begrudge him that before returning to the home ranch.

He had no wish to get into any more conversations. The two jaspers sauntered over and stood next to him, quickly stymying that notion.

One was a hard-nosed jasper sporting a scar above his left eye. His sidekick was a greaser. The two men quickly reduced the level of the bottle of whiskey they had bought. Scarface was clearly the boss. And he was intent on regaling anyone in the immediate vicinity about how he was going to make some dude pay for killing his brother. Fetterman tried to ignore the drunken harangue.

It was only when the name of the Reno Kid cropped up that he took any notice.

'That son-of-the-Devil killed Frank,' the heavily soused bruiser spat out. 'The poor sap stood no chance against a top gun hand like Reno. But he made a big mistake getting involved with a Quintel.' The outlaw wagged a finger and nodded. 'Yep he sure did. And he let slip where he was headed. Maverick. So that's where we're headed. Me and my buddy Fernando here.' A casual arm was draped around his partner's shoulders. 'Then I'll finish the skunk off. And Jeb Quintel will become the dude who bested the Reno Kid.'

A satisfied smirk graced the hard features as he tossed down another slug of hooch. Having finished his slurred delivery, Quintel turned back to the bar and ordered another bottle. Fetterman was thinking hard. His brow furrowed in puzzled concentration. The Reno Kid was supposed to be dead. Some guy had ridden into Maverick over six months before claiming that he had witnessed the renowned bounty hunter's demise at the hands of a cowpoke in St Elmo.

Yet here was a guy squashing all that alleging Reno had shot his brother only days before at the Happy Jack Trading Post. It didn't make no sense. Somebody had to be wrong. The burly cowboy turned to address Jeb Quintel.

'I thought the Reno Kid was dead,' he said, careful

not to appear bellicose. 'Some guy has been spreading the rumour that he was shot up in St Elmo.'

'You calling me a liar, mister?' Quintel's tone was aggressive and challenging.

'No, of course not.' Fetterman backtracked hurriedly in an effort to calm the fractious drinker. 'Just saying what I'd heard, is all.'

'Well I can tell you, fella,' Quintel jabbed a finger into the cowboy's chest, 'the Reno Kid is alive and well. Too darned well. And he's heading for Maverick. But not for long.' An ugly snort meant to be a laugh rumbled up from his throat. 'Ain't that right, Fern?'

'Sure ees, *patrón*,' the Mexican agreed. 'Reno. He not know yet. But his time ees running short.'

Fetterman was stunned. So who was this guy Luther Duggan? And why had he claimed the Reno Kid was dead?'

To make certain he had all the facts correct, Fetterman asked his neighbour to explain what had happened. Quintel was more than willing to expand on the recent incident at the Happy Jack – although he conveniently brushed over the killings at the horse ranch and the humiliating loss of footwear.

'That jasper is gonna rue the day he went up against my kin,' he boasted. 'Next time any of you turkeys hear the name of the Reno Kid, it will be how Jeb Quintel took him down.'

The name of the infamous bounty hunter had brought a gasp from the assembled throng. Quintel smiled. He revelled in the notoriety that his self-assured claim had produced.

'How you gonna do it Jeb?' asked one interested spectator. 'I heard the Reno Kid is faster than a bolt of lightning.'

Quintel sniggered, then tapped his bulbous snout. 'I've said too much already, boys. It don't pay to divulged trade secrets. But what I can say is. . . .'

Buzz Fetterman was not listening. Any thoughts he had harboured about spending some time in Safford were ditched. This was startling news that had to be delivered forthwith. And only he was privy to the show-down that was surely looming. Without further ado, he tossed down the remains of his drink and hurriedly departed.

The ride back to Maverick was undertaken in double-quick time. Only stopping for calls of nature, the cowboy pushed his mount to the limit. It was well lathered and almost fit to drop when he finally stum-bled to a halt outside the Buckeye. Leaping from the saddle, he hustled into the saloon.

Fetterman was enjoying the attention that his out-pouring had engendered. Another drink came his way, which was downed with relish. All eyes were focused on the speaker. It was a rare event for a humble cowhand to be the centre of attention. And he was making the most of it.

Then slowly, one or two eyes gingerly swung towards the man sitting at the back of the room. Most were aware that he had just brought back Luther Duggan, who was now languishing in the jail.

But not everybody was aware of Cole Rickard's infa-mous past. Five years had passed and there were many newcomers who had chosen to settle in the locality in and around Maverick. Henry Cumstick was not the only one to recognize its potential as a fine place in which to live and raise a family.

But all that could be put in jeopardy when Jeb Quintel arrived seeking revenge.

Buzz Fetterman gulped as his gaze followed that of the other patrons. He had not realized the object of his excited outpouring was in the saloon. His face assumed a rosy hue. 'I . . I didn't know you was. . . .'

'Ain't your doing, Buzz,' Digweed placated the contrite cowboy. 'But if'n I was you, I'd drink up and head back to the ranch.'

Fetterman nodded and quickly left.

Cole ignored the cowboy's mumbled apology. He had more important matters to consider. Somehow, Quintel and his buddy must have found some horses. So what had happened to the third outlaw? More important, though, how had he known to head for Maverick? Then he remembered, cursing his over-active mouth. Once again the Reno Kid's reputation for violent gunplay was harrying his trail.

Seemed like he was stuck with it like fleas on a dog's back.

And that is what Marcia clearly felt also. She leapt to her feet glaring at the man her disdainful gaze now accused of duplicity.

'Nothing has changed, has it?' To Cole's ears the leaden charge, flat and lacking any venom sounded worse than any virulent outburst. 'The same old Cole Rickard, the same old reputation following you about like a bad cough.' But it was the next snipe that really cut to the chase. 'You're no better than the deceitful fraud who sought to replace you.'

'But Marcia, I—'

A raised hand chopped off any denial on his part. 'There's nothing can change the way you are. It seems that there will always be somebody willing and eager to challenge the Reno Kid. What Buzz Fetterman said is ample proof of that. I am going now. And I don't want anything more to do with you. Try to contact me or Joey and I will report you to the sheriff for harassment.'

Once again he tried explaining. 'My reasons for coming here are genuine, Marcia. I truly have changed.' He spread his arms apart. 'No guns. Those days are over.'

'But they're not, are they?' The stinging rebuttal struck him in the face, such was its venomous outcome. Marcia's eyes now blazed with fury. 'And they never will be. If that was the case, this man Quintel would not be after you for killing his brother. Are you saying he's mistaken?'

'No, but it wasn't my fault, he—'

'It never is your fault, Cole.' She made to turn her back on this man to whom she had once given her heart. 'There is nothing more to be said. So don't try and follow me. It's over. Goodbye, Cole.'

Tears welled in her eyes. In the course of little over an hour, the two men in her life had let her down badly. One a lowlife fraud, the other a bounty hunter who was destined to live and die by the gun no matter what.

139

Cole was stunned. His eyes followed Marcia as she left the saloon, in essence disappearing out of his life. He was sorely tempted to rush out and plead his case.

'Not now, Cole.' It was the calmly logical voice of Harry Donovan. 'Give her time. Perhaps she'll come round having slept on it. This isn't your fault. I know that. But women always did let their hearts rule their actions.'

'Trouble is, Harry. Time ain't on my side.' Cole was starring at the clock on the wall, the measured swing of the pendulum a constant reminder of the imminent showdown. 'If what that cowboy said is true, those jaspers will be here tomorrow and I'll have to face them down.' He poured out a glass of whiskey and knocked it back. The bite of hard spirit did nothing to assuage his gloom.

Cole's assessment of his adversary's arrival would have been correct had not Jeb Quintel made a detour to Pima Pass. His intention had been to forget about the intended robbery and head directly for Maverick. It was Fernando who urged caution regarding such a provocative action.

'Thee boys will not be pleased that you forsake thees job,' he warned as they left the Wayfarer in Safford.

'Who cares what those goons think?' Quintel bristled indignantly, fixing his sidekick with a caustic glower. 'I'm bossing this outfit. They'll do as I think fit. Anyway, there'll be another payroll along next month. We can do that one. Getting the Reno Kid out of my hair has to take priority.'

The Mexican knew that he had to tread carefully when contradicting Quintel. He might easily treat it as a personal affront, which would be an unhealthy move. Mustang Charlie would have harboured no such qualms, but he was dead. Even so, Estrela decided to push his luck.

'They might well decide to pull job on ownsome,' he speculated. The idea had been broached by Charlie Bassett while they were waiting for Quintel at Happy Jack. Only now had it resurfaced. 'Punk Adler ees not likely to just walk away. And he will persuade the others that they can go it alone. That hombre has always wanted to boss hees own gang. Thees would be chance he has been waiting for.'

Quintel's brain was tossing over the implications of what Estrela had suggested. And it made sense. Adler was a big mouth. Worst than that, he had ambitions. A top gun hand when the chips were down, but not a jigger to cold shoulder. Fernando was right. And so a detour over to Pima Pass was made.

The gang were told that the payroll had been delayed. He softened the grumbling discontent by dipping into his own stash of funds. It was an uncharacteristic gesture, but nobody was about to complain when a few nights of carousel in Benson were in the offing. The gang parted. Even Punk Adler was smiling.

So here they were on the outskirts of Maverick in the San Carlos Valley. A sleepy town where not much was likely to disturb the tranquil ambience. Quintel smiled at the notion. Well, that was about to change big time.

During the ride over from Pima Pass, Quintel had

come to realize that in taking on the Reno Kid man-to-man, there was no certainty he would come out on top. The outlaw boss was a competent gun hand. But there were better. Punk Adler for one, and probably Fernando as well.

Quintel smiled to himself. A coyote's bark displayed more levity. There was always more than one way to skin a cat. Booking a one-way ticket for the bounty man on Boot Hill would require the cunning of a successful owlhooter. Somebody with guile and ingenuity.

That person was Jeb Quintel.

Frank had stood even less chance than he, but hadn't the sense to back off. Although his younger brother had come off worse in the confrontation at Happy Jack, Quintel was secretly glad. Of course he would never confess to such an admission, even to himself; kinship pride demanded an eye for an eye.

But with Frank out of the running, the road was left wide open for him to step in and claim the prize. In his own devious way.

'I'm going in alone,' he informed his sidekick. 'You stay here while I take care of things.' Quintel had expected Fernando to object but had his reply ready. 'I have to face him alone. Folks need to see that Jeb Quintel has made his play in time honoured fashion and come out the winner.'

'*Sí, patrón*. I understand.' The need to prove one's *masculinidad* was a powerful force in every Mexican male. There was no more to be said.

Jeb Quintel nudged his horse towards the town.

Cole was idly playing patience in the Buckeye. Any

attempt at conversation was brusquely rebuffed. He was becoming ever more tetchy as the time passed with no sign of Quintel. He had no doubt that the guy would show. Perhaps he was playing the waiting game to unnerve and demoralize his opponent. Well, it was working.

Each resonant hourly toll of the clock set his nerves on edge. And his mouth felt sour like there was something dead inside.

He called across to the barman. 'Hey, Digweed, you got some buttermilk around?'

The tapster's heavy brows lifted at the unusual request. 'Reckon I can run some to earth, Mr Rickard,' he replied. He disappeared out back returning moments later with a jug and glass, which he deposited in front of Cole. A glass was poured but the contents left untouched.

A down-at-heel prospector had just shambled through the door and called out. 'Anybody in here by the name of Rickard?'

Cole instantly threw off his inertia and stood up. 'Over here, mister.'

The milk was forgotten as the old dude wandered over and handed him a note. 'Fella said you'd give me some'n for my trouble.'

'Did this guy have a scar above his left eye?' snapped Cole before reading the note.

'That's him. A right shifty character,' snorted the oldster. 'And he was packing a brace of pistols in a fancy rig as well.'

Cole flipped a silver dollar in the air, which the

prospector caught with nonchalant ease. A quick bite to check it was genuine, then he moved across to the bar.

Opening the note, Cole read the scrawled words to himself.

'Is it from this guy Jeb Quintel?' inquired Flush Harry, who had sidled up behind his buddy. Cole nodded. He handed the note across. It read: *At end of China Alley. Come alone. And bring a gun.* It was not signed. There was no need.

'You keep out of this, Harry. It's between me and destiny.' He gripped his old pal's hand firmly. Then, in words barely above a whisper, avowed, 'It's gonna be the last time. Of that I can promise you. And tell Marcia that I'll always love her and little Joey, no matter what.'

FOURTEEN

NO WAY BACK

Strange words. Almost like an epitaph. Harry Donovan frowned in puzzlement as his friend left the saloon.

Settling the belt and holster on his hip, Cole Rickard, the Reno Kid, headed for China Alley. There was nobody on the street. It was as if the whole town sensed that trouble of a violent nature was brewing. Cole moved into the centre of the thoroughfare and slowly began the walk of providence.

China Alley was a narrow passage between a Chinese laundry and the Lotus Flower Oriental Eatery. The name was depicted in Chinese characters with its English equivalent underneath. Cole paused at the entrance. The sun failed to penetrate the gloomy passageway.

Loosening his six-shooter, Cole started down the narrow opening. A cat squealed, then darted out beneath his feet.

Halfway down, he stopped and called out. 'Show yourself, Quintel, and let's get this business settled once and for all.'

'It's already settled, Reno.' The gruff declaration was punched out from a dim recess. It was followed by a loud report and a flash of orange. Two bullets struck Cole high up in the chest. 'And I'm the winner.' A surly chortle followed the downed man as he slumped to the ground.

Quintel stepped out of the shadows and walked across to the crumpled form. An ugly grin split the harsh features. A thin beam of sunlight glanced off the bushwacker's taut features as he stared down at the man he had shot.

The victim of the cowardly ambush groaned. Quintel stepped back, fleetingly nonplussed. He pointed his gun at the dying man ready to deliver the coup de grace. But another voice stayed the Reaper's hand.

'Pull that trigger and it'll be the last thing you do, mister.' The blunt promise came from the lips of Sheriff Chalk Fenton. 'You're under arrest for murder. Now drop the gun.'

'It was a fair fight, Sheriff. Me and this dude had things to settle.' Quintel was sweating in the cool of China Alley. 'I didn't force him down here. He came of his own accord.'

Quintel was taken aback by the lawman's unex- pected appearance. Fenton had been checking on a mundane complaint about rubbish left behind the Chinese laundry when the shooting started. He ignored the plea of innocence. His own gun rose menacingly. 'Drop the hogleg. I won't tell you again.'

The shooter hit the ground with a dull thud. It was then that the fallen man pushed himself up on one elbow. 'It's true what he said, Sheriff,' Cole blurted out gasping for breath. He was clearly far gone.

'Easy there, mister. You need a doctor.'

'No time for that. We did have things to settle. And he beat me fair and square. But it was me that drew first.' Cole coughed out a plume of blood. The final curtain was about to fall. All three of them knew it.

'I don't need your help, Reno,' growled the killer.

Cole forced a smile. 'This ain't help, Quintel. It's a curse that's gonna haunt you for what little time you have left. You're now the gunnie who shot the Reno Kid.' He stopped to get his breath back. 'And it's a heavy burden to tote around. Young punks like Frank are gonna be out to test you and claim the crown. . . .' A macabre guffaw rattled in his throat. More blood issued from the open mouth. 'A crown of thorns, more like. Look at me good, mister. And see yourself in a month or two, maybe even a year if'n you're lucky.'

He sank back. The effort of his final denouement too much. His eyes blinked once then closed. Cole Rickard and the Reno Kid were no more.

At that moment, Flush Harry dashed down the alley. 'What's happened?' he demanded. Then seeing his friend on the ground, he hurried across and bent down.

'Is he. . . ?'

'Afraid so, Harry,' the lawman replied. 'And apparently it was a fair fight. This guy beat the Reno Kid to the draw.' He pointed to the revolver clutched in the dead man's hand. At some point following the shooting, Cole had drawn his pistol to add credence to his interpretation that it had been a fair showdown.

Witnessing Quintel's unctuous smirk, Harry slammed a bunched fist into the killer's face. The outlaw was caught unawares by the sudden move and went down. A brutal kick in the ribs followed it up. Harry was fuming and ready to administer more of the same. Quintel rolled away to escape the furious assault.

'Get him off'n me, Sheriff. I ain't done nothing wrong,' he whined.

Fenton sensed that all was not as it appeared. But he had no proof that the Kid's version of events was not the truth.

'OK, Harry, let him alone,' the sheriff ordered laying a firm hand on the assailant's arm. 'I'll deal with this. Before passing away, Reno admitted to me that he drew first. So there's nothing I can do if'n this guy ain't broken the law.'

'You can't hold him. Is that what you're saying?' exclaimed the outraged saloon owner. 'It ain't right. He's a durned murderer.'

Fenton shrugged. 'That ain't what the law says. My hands are tied. And until an ordnance is passed prohibiting the wearing of firearms within the town limits, all I can do is make sure the critter leaves town.'

Like numerous other lawmen throughout Arizona, Chalk Fenton had warrants for the arrest of the gang known as the Shadow Riders. But the name of Jeb Quintel and a solid and reliable description were

148

distinctly lacking. He had no idea, therefore, of the true identity of this unsavoury character.

He then turned to address the alleged winner of the contest, who was wiping blood from a pulped mouth. 'There'll be no more gunplay in Maverick while I'm in charge, mister. So I advise you to get out while you can. News of this nature gets around mighty fast. And I can think of two young hotheads hereabouts who'd love to go up agin the slick gunhand who bested the Reno Kid.'

Quintel scrambled to his feet and snatched up his hat. He was about to retrieve his revolver when the lawman snapped. 'Leave it! You can make do with the other one. Now git afore I change my mind.'

A thoroughly chastened Jeb Quintel mounted up and swung away. He had much to think on before returning to his waiting buddy on the edge of town. A story had to be hastily concocted to ensure he emerged from the fracas in a good light. The bleeding mouth could be explained away easily enough.

The gunfire in China Alley had attracted a host of onlookers. Craning necks sought to peer into the gloomy passage.

'What was all the gunplay about?' posed one jigger.

'Seems like there's been a shoot-out.'

'Who between?'

One boastful strutter who seemed to know more than others provided enlightenment. 'The Reno Kid's been shot dead.' Gasps of awed shock at this momentous news rustled through the gathering throng.

'I thought he was dead already,' said a grizzled war veteran.

'He came back here after five years away up north.'

'What about that Irish jasper who ingratiated himself into Marcia Rickard's bed? Guess he wasn't too happy.'

And so it went on. Numerous theories were latched onto and discarded as the crowd surged back and forth. Each neck-stretcher hoping to discover the truth and pass it on. Information like that was always worth a few free drinks for the informant.

A wagon driven by Harvey Cumstick pulled up at the edge of the crowd. 'What's all the fuss?' he inquired of the nearest bystander.

'There's been a gunfight.'

'Anyone killed?'

'They say that the Reno Kid has been bested by some tearaway,' was the knowledgeable reply.

'I thought he was dead,' said a bewildered Cumstick.

'So did everybody else. Guess we were wrong. And it also seems like his real name was Rickard. Cole Rickard.'

Cumstick gasped aloud. 'I was only talking to that guy a few days past. Reckoned he was fixing to settle down here.'

The informant responded with an ironic chortle. 'He's sure done that but in a place he never expected.' Cumstick gave the remark a quizzical frown. 'The graveyard, where else?'

The tit-for-tat discourse was cut short when the crowd parted to allow a solitary female to pass down the alley. Knowing elbows nudged into ribs as Marcia Rickard gingerly neared the scene of sudden and violent death. She came to a halt on seeing the blood-stained body of her husband. Overcome by grief, she clutched at an iron downspout. And would have collapsed had not Harry Donovan quickly stepped forward to hold her upright.

'I'm sorry, Marcia,' he mumbled inanely. 'Guess his time had come. He knew it would one day.'

The woman remained silent. Her face a white mask. A single teardrop chased a path down a smooth cheek. She quickly brushed it away. Why had she not stuck by him? Other questions filtered through her distraught brain, all encompassed by the guilt that now assailed her whole being.

This was the only man she had ever loved. Or ever would. Life had dealt them both a poor hand. She watched as the undertaker carefully loaded the shattered corpse onto a wagon, and covered it with a black cloth. It slowly moved away. Assisted by Harry Donovan, she followed behind, head bowed. Pain and anguish were written indelibly across her ashen face.

Aveline Beddows joined her, murmuring endearments.

It was three days later that the funeral cortege made its way to the small graveyard on a hill overlooking Maverick. A couple of limp palo verde trees and some wild roses attempted to break the austere nature of the bleak site. A grave had already been dug at one end where the preacher stood, Bible in hand.

A light breeze wafted across the open sward rippling leaves on the trees. Cactus wrens chirped and swooped about, unconcerned by the sober occasion taking place in their midst. There was a surprisingly large turnout. Those who had known the deceased took frontal positions around the empty hole. Others were merely curious, eager to follow the final moments of the infamous bounty hunter.

The low babble of conversation faded as the preacher began intoning the funeral dirge. His flat delivery was awkward and strained for a man who had never personally known the coffin's incumbent.

Following the burial, most of the gathering departed. There was food and drink available at the Buckeye that nobody wanted to miss.

Left behind were the nearest and dearest. Marcia had reverted to her true married name. Her marriage to Lex Dooley, or was it Luther Duggan, had been a sham. Young Joey clutched her hand. He had never really known his father. So the man in the grave was a stranger.

'Your pa loved you, Joey,' his mother intoned struggling to keep the grief from her voice. 'He wanted only the best for you. Promise me that you'll always look on Cole Rickard as your true father.' For the last few years, the charlatan known as Luther Duggan had played that part surprisingly well. Now he was in jail awaiting collection for trial in Colorado.

The boy's response was a brief nod. His whole world had been turned upside down.

'He will live on in our memories.' Marcia gripped his hand firmly. 'And this grave is a reminder of all he meant to us both. Make sure that you visit it often.'

Even though there was no way back for the Reno Kid in this life, perhaps he would now be reconciled with his loved ones in their hearts as well as the hereafter.

FIFTEEN

FINALE

Three weeks after the burial of the Reno Kid in Maverick, the Shadow Riders led by Jeb Quintel were concealed behind some rocks at Pima Pass. The monthly payroll to Fort Defiance was due any minute. Tension gripped the participants. The gang boss had gained added celebrity amongst his men after relating his own version of the events leading to the shoot-out at Maverick.

Being the man who had taken down the Reno Kid and satisfied family honour sat well on his shoulders. The robbery would cement his reputation amongst others of like mind.

The only burr in the ointment was Punk Adler. The guy had not made any overtly disparaging comments, but the sour looks when he thought the boss was not watching had made Quintel suspicious of his intentions. He pledged to chop the guy down to size once this caper was over and they were in the clear.

The wagon containing the strongbox was escorted by four troopers. Moments later it appeared in the mouth of the pass. A deep rift in the Swisshelm Mountains, this was the only feasible route for a wagon travelling from Tucson to the army fort.

The Shadows were well hidden amongst the rocks on either side of the trail. Quintel was always the one to set the ball rolling. He waited until the wagon was well into the pass. A raised hand signalled the onset of the heist.

His rifle instantly belched flame and death. One of the troopers was lifted from the saddle. The rest of the gang opened up. In no time the three other guards quickly followed. At the top end of the pass, three more men jumped out in front of the careering wagon. The driver and his associate knew better than to resist. They drew the rig to a stumbling halt.

Quintel smiled to himself as he emerged from cover. Easy as falling off a log.

'Glad you boys saw sense,' he praised the two survivors. Then to his men. 'Throw that box down and let's see what we have here.'

Two bullets smashed the iron lock. Inside were stacked wads of greenbacks, ten thousand dollars in total according to his informant – the company payroll clerk. Quintel riffled through a pack of notes and peeled off a handful, which he handed to the driver. 'Your reward for not causing us any trouble. Don't spend it all in the same saloon, boys.'

Then he slapped the lead cayuse on the rump. The

animal jerked forward. The eight Shadows chuckled uproariously as the driver struggled to get his rig back under control. Neither of the two men looked back. The money they had been given was more than three months' wages for each of them. And they intended keeping it.

As with other previously successful raids in the vicinity, the gang retired to Happy Jack for the all-important share out. A couple of days spent at the trading post then the gang split up to go their separate ways. There was enough dough for each man to enjoy a fine spree in the flesh pots of Mexico for a few months.

'We'll meet up back here in November,' said Quintel.

'Where you headed, boss?' Punk Adler asked casually.

'Figure I'll trail down to Nogales where gals are cheap and the boozed is even cheaper.' He chuckled at the notion. 'You up for that, Fernando?'

'That ees good thinking, *patron*. I introduce you to my *parientes*. They make you very welcome.'

Adler joined in. 'Sounds good. Maybe I'll join you. I can't allow the guy who shot the Reno Kid to get himself into bother.' The smile seemed genuine, but the eyes remained cold and granite hard.

Quintel gave nothing away but he knew what game Adler was playing and would be ready when the skunk made his move.

The expected confrontation came sooner than expected. They were camped out that same night beside Boulder Creek en route to the silver boomtown of Tombstone. Quintel was poking at a rabbit that was being spit roasted over the fire. Fernando had gone down to the creek for water. The two men were alone.

'Me and the boys have been talking,' Adler growled. 'We figure you're past it, Jeb. Toting that Reno reputation around ain't good for business. It will attract too much attention, which the Shadows don't need.'

Quintel maintained a calm head. Without looking up his reply was icy cool and measured. 'And I suppose you're the guy that thinks he can take over.'

'Why not? I can out gun you anytime.'

Slowly, Quintel rose to his feet and turned to face his adversary. 'Then let's not waste any time. You want to boss this outfit? Then you'll have to get rid of me first. And I ain't volunteering. So you best put up, or shut up.'

Punk Adler was puzzled. His broad forehead crinkled. He knew for a fact that he could beat Quintel to the draw. Only the guy's talent for nosing out good jobs had stayed his hand thus far. But now ruthless ambition to lead and ride up front had propelled him to take this decisive action.

He hesitated. Quintel sneered. 'Scared that you ain't as good as you figured. Is that it, Punk?'

The pretender to the outlaw throne growled. His hand dropped to the gun on his hip. But it never lifted. His mouth opened wide in shock, then looked down at the tip of a large knife protruding from his belly.

'There ees only one leader of thee Shadows and it ees not you, hombre.' Fernando had known all along of Adler's surreptitious intentions. The pair had deliberately engineered this situation to draw him out.

157

'Well that sure worked to perfection, Fern,' Quintel gushed as Adler slumped to the floor. 'A guy doesn't always have to be the fastest draw in the West to gain an enviable reputation.'

'You are right there, *patron*.' A sinister twinkle burned in the Mexican's eyes. 'A man needs brains and cunning. Plus a ruthless streak, I theenk.' His gun rose and pumped two bullets into the smiling face of Jeb Quintel. 'Now I, Fernando Estrela, can finally return to my homeland, head held high and with a reputation to match.'

Quintel lurched forward, unable to comprehend what was happening. The rictus of death stared him in the face. A groping hand clutched at thin air. Suddenly a light dawned in the dying man's watery eyes.

But it was too late for Jeb Quintel, who tried to speak but couldn't. His killer looked askance, unable to comprehend what the dying man was trying to say.

A year had passed since the morose burial of Cole Rickard. Life in Maverick had settled down to much as it was before. Flush Harry Donovan was sitting in the Palace Hotel awaiting the afternoon stagecoach from Tucson. He was expecting the arrival of a leading lady who had been booked for a two week performance at the Buckeye.

The stage was due in ten minutes. Sipping at his coffee, he idly perused the latest edition of the *Bisbee Herald*. It had been left by a travelling salesman in barbershop accoutrements. A heading at the bottom of the page caught his eye.

Slowly he read the article. Eyes bulged wide as the import of the news struck home.

FAMOUS GUNFIGHTER SHOT
RESISTING ARREST

Yesterday, the renowned Mexican gunslinger, Fernando Estrela, was shot dead on the main street of Bisbee when he refused to surrender his guns. An ordnance recently enacted to combat lawless brigands from south of the border forbade the wearing of firearms within the town limits. Estrela had objected, taunting Marshal Sam Grover to remove them if he had the nerve.

Estrela had been drinking. The marshal gave the gunslinger ample opportunity to obey the order, but the gunman refused, claiming the man who held the reputation for killing the infamous Reno Kid had every right to bear arms where and whenever he chose. A further attempt to defuse the rapidly escalating showdown proved fruitless. Estrela was intent on enhancing his infamous reputation at any cost. Even if it meant going up against a lawman.

He went to draw his gun, but drink had slowed his reactions. Marshal Grover was given no option but to draw his own pistol and shoot the man. Before he passed away, the gunman was heard to mutter the words:

'Now I understand what you mean about the curse, Jeb.' Everybody was mystified regarding this strange dying announcement. If any readers can provide enlightenment, the editor of the *Bisbee Herald* would be eager to hear from them.

Numerous reports had come down the grapevine of gunslingers allegedly claiming to have shot the Reno Kid. All had proved to be fictitious. But this one appeared to be genuine. Jeb Quintel had done the actual shooting but he was known to have a Mexican sidekick. Mention of a curse further added credence to the report. Estrela must have got rid of the outlaw leader and assumed the mantle himself.

Perhaps now the curse of the fast gun could finally be laid to rest. Like all the others before him, Fernando Estrela had learned too late that for those who live by the gun there can indeed be *No Way Back*.